Lexie

Thanks for your

support. Best

Wish

7/16/04

READERS REVIEW for
SOILED PILLOWCASES

"**STANDING OVATION** for the passionately, soul stirring novel..... **Soiled Pillowcases.** Newcomer author Crystal Stell vivaciously jumps on the novelist scene and makes her presence known! **Soiled Pillowcases** is a captivating, provocative account that examines the realism of the lessons of life, relationships, love, success, and happiness. Author Stell skillfully offers her readers an intriguing odyssey of the physical and emotional skeletons that gradually begin to creep out of an unlocked closet."
Leslie Lewis, Evangelist
Chicago, Illinois

"**WOW!** Crystal has begun her literary career with a BANG! It is almost hard to believe that this is her very first novel. Readers are sure to be surprised as they read this novel. It had me in awe and on an emotional roller coaster from beginning to the end. It was difficult for me to put down and I anxiously await Crystal's sophomore project. Job well done."
Victor Cheatham, Educational Administrator
Dallas, Texas

"Soiled Pillowcases was a great read. I am not a fan of fiction, but I found myself deeply interested in the characters. I was drawn into the story and could actually feel the character's anxiety. I appreciated the use of real settings and could feel the atmosphere of each moment. It's a great book Crystal. **Outstanding Job**, I commend you on your efforts for your freshman project."
Marc Flemon, Academic Advisor
Detroit, Michigan

"Crystal This is an excellent, excellent book. I enjoyed reading it, it kept my interest and kept me in suspense. Soiled Pillowcases had all the elements of a great book."
Dr. JoAnn Clark, Author
Langston, Oklahoma

"BRAVO!!!!!!!!!!!! Soiled Pillowcases was so AWESOME. I could relate to the main character, Kyra Murrell. Talk about becoming a part of the novel. Chapters 7 through 21 were excellent. I read all of those chapters in one sitting because I couldn't put the book down."
Anitra Rivers, Day Care Operator
Oklahoma City, Oklahoma

"Mrs. Stell, this is a wonderful book. Men and women can truly relate to this novel because it is so realistic. Soiled Pillowcases is going to be a BEST SELLER."
Jacaria Linder, College Student
Los Angeles, California

"Any person that has ever been in a relationship and experienced any kind of trials or tribulations can relate to this novel. This book provides a realistic approach to dealing with a troubled relationship. I loved it, I could relate to it and I'm going to refer it to some of my friends and family."
Bonita Camacho, College Student
Las Vegas, Nevada

"Realistic, and good therapy for me. I could see my current relationship, and myself many times, throughout this story. I've been inspired by this novel to examine myself, and consider ways I can improve as a mate. "
Abraham Gordon, Engineer
Brooklyn, New York

Soiled Pillowcases

A Married Woman's Story

Crystell Publications

Oklahoma   Detroit   Atlanta   D.C.   Dallas   Virginia

Soiled Pillowcases

A Married Woman's Story

BY: Crystal Perkins-Stell

First Printing   2003

Cover Designed by: Harold Gains
Gaines@hj-inc.com

Web Site Designed by: Samuel Graham III
Sgraham@internetlords.net

To place an order contact: **www.Crystalstell.com**

PUBLISHED BY: *CRYSTELL PUBLICATIONS*
P.O. BOX 8044
EDMOND, OK. 73083-8044

ISBN: 0-9740705-6-4
Library of Congress Control Number: 2003094370

Printed in the United States of America

Dedicated to Makya Alexis
my beautiful 2-year-old Diamond in the raw.
God blessed me when He made you a part of my life.
I pray that I will always be the example you look to for your
Role Model.
May you always be proud to refer to me as your
MOM.

God bless you baby; mommy loves you.
Smooches

"Sometimes when your life is lacking something you feel you need, deserve, or want, it is virtually impossible at times to just do without."

Quote by Kyra Murrell

Contents

ACKNOWLEDGEMENTS
INTRODUCTION

Chapters

Acknowledgements

First and foremost, I'd like to thank God for blessing me with a gift. It is because of Him that I am the person I have become, and to Him, I give all the honor and glory.

There are so many other people I'd like to thank for supporting me, while I worked on this book. Damon Stell, thanks for being patient when I was totally engaged in creating, and neglected to prepare you dinner. Karolyn Lewis, mom, thanks for encouraging me when I felt most discouraged. Thanks for being my friend and my shoulder when I needed to vent about the stressors of self-publishing, and when my computer dumped twenty-five pages of edited material. You may never realize how much I appreciate you for reading and re-reading "Soiled Pillowcases." I love you so much for believing in me and teaching me to follow the desires of my heart.

Miles, Marcus, and Kimberly Lewis, my siblings, thanks for inspiring me. Yeah, even though you only want my book to be a "Best-Seller" for personal gain. (Smile) Moses Washington, thanks for trying to understand fatherhood. Grandma Mae Washington, Love You, Mean It. (Peace) Mike May, Dawn Perkins, and T. Bell, thanks for reading my first four original chapters of my book and motivating me to continue on with vigor. Gabriel, (G.G.), know that real friendships and diamonds have something in common; they are forever. Thanks for your listening ear. Iris Thompson thanks for being the first person to completely read my book and provide me with my first critique. Tommy Dunn, thank you for your idea for a book cover. Jean Wise, thank you for openly sharing your experiences as a first time author. I wish you much success with your first novel.

I must also thank some wonderful students at Langston University. Angela Austin, Jeffery Stevenson, Jertonya Feemster, Joe Gibson, KP, Jacari, Bonita, Gi., and Barry Jones. Thanks for nagging me to death about finishing "The Book." You'd better get ready to help make sales happen. Sam Graham III, thanks for creating my logo and website, **www.crystalstell.com**. I know that I got on your last nerve sometimes talking about Crystell Publications. Mr. Lawrence, you have believed in me since day one. Thanks for helping me believe that I could fly. Chirice Storr, you are the bomb girl, thanks for everything. Harvey and Ben, who knows what tomorrow brings? Lawanda Watts-Burley, I'm so grateful for our renewed friendship. You have been a beaming light in my life and a true example of what real friends are made of.. Mark Storey and TAGG, my ability to create started way back in middle school when our friendships were blossoming. Allen Whitsett, you better read the book, and get ready for me to tell your awesome story. Monty and Scooter, thanks for your love, and support in everything I do. You guys certainly know how to make a cousin feel special. Keep Shining! No matter what, I love you guys so much.

Harold Gaines, thank you so much for my cover, **I LOVE IT.** Mary Ellen, thanks for the academic collegiate level critique on my novel. Anthony Hill thanks for sending them my way. Deborah Jackson and Victor Cheatham thanks, for your wonderful friendship. You guys have been there for me since forever. Best wishes to you and your families. I love you guys so much. Jackie P., and Kishmar, hope you like my book. Leigh Gilkey, thanks for coming through for me when I needed you. Fred Moulder, thanks for your input on things sly brothers try to pull on sistas. Thanks the Stell family. And a super thanks to my sorority sisters, who have been very supportive of me…the illustrious women of Delta Sigma Theta Sorority Inc., Chris, Monique, and Christopher Horton Jr., Shelly Coleman, Keshondra Young, Darren in H-Town, Mark F., and Tara, thanks for your encouragement.

I'd like to say thank you in advance to all of the book clubs and dedicated readers who have purchased my book and supported me in my efforts to successfully accomplish my dream. I appreciate you and will never forget the way you embraced me as a new author.

Finally, I would also like to thank Mr. Tom Joyner. In 2001, he delivered Langston University's Commencement Address. He asked the graduating class, "What you gon' do now?" As I attentively listened to him, I thought of how hectic it must have been for him to fulfill his fulltime Disc Jockey obligations in Dallas and Chicago. I considered the dedication and determination his goals required and knew that I too had the necessary talent to make my dreams a reality. His speech was very inspirational, and though I was not a graduate, Tom Joyner motivated me to stop **talking** about my dreams and **start living them to the fullest.**

So to the **hardest working D.J. in radio**, I say thank you so much.

Introduction

Topics regarding relationships are one of the most controversial subjects we encounter during co-ed discussions. I have engaged in group discussions with individuals of various socioeconomic backgrounds regarding relationships for years. What I have discovered is that males and females, regardless of their age groups, fail to completely understand why the other operates in the manner in which they do. However, men and woman alike are looking for complete fulfillment in the person they label as their soul mate. Is there such a thing as "complete fulfillment" from someone of the opposite sex? I believe that this kind of relationship is possible when the lines of communication are of high quality.

Most often when we initially date, we find ourselves head over heels in love with our significant other. But, somewhere down the line, for some reason or another, feelings change and relationships go from wonderful to a living nightmare. One of the biggest issues plaguing relationships in society today is infidelity. As common as infidelity is, one might simply view it as just the way we operate in this era. But, it is a contagious epidemic far greater than what we give it credit for. Infidelity causes a compromise of ones morals, self-respect, families, and, sometimes lives.

Individuals dating in society today are not modeling appropriate, healthy dating techniques. Therefore, the formula for maintaining a healthy relationship is not being taught for future improvement to our offspring and future leaders. If there is ever to be a successful formula for relationships, we must first examine ourselves, then groom our minds to focus on understanding the way our mates think, and what truly makes them happy.

Soiled Pillowcases has a fictitious storyline based on the realistic problems men and women face when looking for love outside of their marriage or committed relationship. Many fail to realize, while reaping the benefits of their affair, that they only serve as temporary resolutions. However, to some degree, great losses and heartaches are generally the outcome, once exposed. This book was written to provide readers with a superficial, but quite realistic example of how affairs destroy homes. I hope this novel inspires men and women to examine their behavior and work on resolving adversities in their relationship long before they result in deception or divorce.

1

Bitter As Hell

Kyra Murrell sat in her living room daydreaming of how she would finally share her story of an extramarital affair with members in her Divorce and Marital Misconduct Group. After staring into space for over twenty minutes, she was startled by the sudden beeping of her cell phone alarm. It was automatically programmed to beep bi-weekly, which served as a reminder for her Friday morning therapy session.

Kyra slowly pulled herself up from the couch, grabbing her purse and keys. As she shut the door behind her, she listened for the beeping of the house alarm to ensure that it set correctly. She pushed the opener to the garage and watched as it slowly rose. "Damn, I should just stay home today," she stated, while walking to her car. "But then you'd never move on with your life and forgive Bruce or yourself," her conscience quickly replied. "You're right," she stated, as she put her gear in reverse, backed out of the driveway and drove to her group session.

Kyra arrived at the counseling center early. She poured herself a glass of orange juice and sat in a chair in the back of the room. She looked around the empty room, envisioning it full of people and her heart began to pound. She had finally convinced herself that she would share her story with the group, and the anxiety of telling her dark secret overwhelmed her. She had always been quite reserved about divulging her personal business, but for the sake of saving her family, she was going to share her story, release the guilt she carried daily and attempt to get on with her life.

Minutes later, other group members started arriving. As the group facilitator entered the room, he closed the door behind him.

"Good morning everyone. Wasn't that some kind of session we had two weeks ago. I hope you all thought about some of the issues we addressed and are ready to get down to business again this morning?" he stated, while looking around the room at everyone. Kyra could hear her heart pounding, as he made direct eye contact with her and asked, "Is there anyone that would like to share anything with the group before we get started?" She instantly began to perspire, as she envisioned the walls caving in on her.

"Is he talking to me," she thought to herself? Then Carla, another group member who had been attending therapy for eleven months, raised her hand. "I would like to share with the group that my husband and I have reconciled our differences, and decided to get back together and work on our marriage once again."

Most of the group started clapping, but Kyra just sat with her arms crossed and looked around the room. Anita, another member noticed her behavior and quickly confronted her.

"What's wrong Kyra? Did you hear Carla's news?" She asked.
"Yes Anita. I sure did."
"Well aren't you happy for her?"
"Sure, I'm happy for her. I guess I just didn't feel much like clapping."
"Well don't you think her news is worth celebrating, since she thought enough of the group to share it with us?"
"Anita, you've been focusing on me for the past few sessions. I feel as though you are trying to intentionally make me look bad to the other group members, and I don't appreciate it. I don't know why you feel like you can question me about my action because I don't owe you or anyone else an explanation for my behavior."
"As long as you are a part of this group, you do owe the members an explanation when someone confronts you."
"Anita, I didn't feel like celebrating Carla's news because right now I'm extremely bitter towards men, poor ass marriages, and making things work. I'm happy for her, but I don't necessarily know if her news is worth celebrating for me. I feel disappointed,

and I'm sorry that my demeanor is not acceptable in your eyes, but it's me and that's that. If you don't like it, don't deal with me. Trust me, we will both get over it."

"Kyra you've been coming to therapy for six months, listening to everyone's story and missing out on your real opportunity to release what you're feeling inside. All you do is shake you head in agreement, and when you speak, you never interject any real input. Most often what you contribute to the groups discussion is very superficial. If you ask me, you're really defeating the purpose of therapy anyway, and wasting your money and our time. So why are you here Kyra, and what are you so bitter about?"

The group facilitator attempted to interrupt the conversation between the two, which appeared to be getting a little heated. As he tries to regain control of the session, Kyra cuts him off.

"I'm bitter because my husband cheated on me and fucked up our marriage. I'm angry with myself because I allowed myself to be suckered into having a rendezvous with a man who forced me to see what I lost in my husband. And, I'm bitter because every day that I think about Everett Barnett, it reminds me of the dark secret I carry daily. I must admit that I thought once I started actively participating in group, I would feel a little better about getting on with my life, but I'm mad as hell about my situation. I'm struggling emotionally, and I'm unable to move on with my life because of the agony I experience daily. You don't know the heartaches I've experienced because of my failed marriage. You don't know how often I lay awake in bed at night wondering why my husband found companionship and comfort in another woman. You don't know the pain I encounter when I look into my three-and-a- half-year-old daughter's eyes and try to explain to her why her mommy and daddy live in separate homes. And, you don't know the countless number of pillowcases I have soiled with tears since I told my husband, Bruce, over a year ago that we needed to separate. You ask why I'm so bitter Anita? Well, why shouldn't I be?"

"Kyra, you haven't said anything that other women in this group aren't going through as well. But we're genuinely trying to help ourselves in order to move on with our lives. And, for the record, you haven't been actively participating. You're harboring ill feelings, concealing your pain, and trying to protect your rich, I done made it over girl image. And that's why you're stuck. What you need to do is stop listening to everyone else's story while hiding behind your elaborate financial status, and start talking about your issues,.......... if you really want to help yourself."

"Anita, my concern is not the other women in this group. My concern is me, my pain and what I can do to get through this."

"Kyra, you get through it by talking about what's causing you so much pain," Anita rudely suggested.

As Kyra looked around the room, tears fell from her eyes. She wiped her face with the palms of her hands, took a deep breath, glanced at the group facilitator for reassurance, and started her story.

My husband, Bruce Murrell, was this wonderfully charming man I met in 1992 at a church basketball tournament. His complexion was silky smooth chocolate, like Morris Chestnuts, and he stood about six feet, five inches tall. He had a closely trimmed mustache and dimples deeper than the Grand Canyon. He was a handsome, professional brotha in his early thirties and had been labeled by female social groups in the community as, "The Catch of the Year." He was a six-digit income; Chemical Engineer for a major oil company based out of Texas and was extremely intellectual. With all this brotha had going for himself, he could have easily been an arrogant, stuck up, Corporate America asshole. But, he was always very charming and quite modest. His personality was warm, and he exemplified a love for God that was contagious.

Women of all ages were very attracted to him. What disgusted me the most was the manner in which single women flocked behind him in the Lord's house. I had never seen anything like it before in my life. And when he purchased his first "A Brotha Done Made It," set of wheels, I thought sistas were going to lose their damn minds.

Actually, after really getting to know Bruce and observing how crazy women really were about him, I made it a point to ensure that I kept our relationship platonic. I did not want my name coming up in conversations amongst the various church gossipers as one of the holy hoochies on his tab. Besides, when we met, I was dating a guy named Calvin, so my interest in Bruce was strictly friendship based.

Though he was highly attracted to me, he respected my commitment, but always told me if I ever broke up with Calvin, "It was over for him." I really just thought he was talking because Calvin and I had been together forever. So, when Bruce and I became real good friends, I focused more on setting him up with a few sista's I worked with to divert his attraction from me. But Bruce was single, lonely, and knew exactly what he was looking for in a woman. So, for a while, none of his blind dates were working out. I agreed to occasionally accompany him out on professional dinner meetings until he found someone special. However, the more I introduced him to potential mates, the more uninterested he became in being set up with other women.

He always teased me about my light greenish-brown eyes and my buttery caramel skin tone, which he believed was a beautiful combination. He assured me that if I could find him a sista that was 5'6, 130 pounds with fine, medium length hair, greenish-brown eyes like mine, and the old school cola bottle figure, he would stop turning down my hook-ups. But, the only sista I knew that fit that description was me, so what was he trying to indirectly say.

Calvin and I started experiencing problems in 1994. He became distracted with night clubbing and titty bar hopping. From there, he started acting crazy, talking crazy, living crazy, and I wasn't having that kind of foolishness or drama in my life. During that time, I was on a mission to refine my character and the woman I was striving to be in life. I had just dedicated my life to Christ and was trying to grow spiritually closer to God. Calvin assured me that he wanted no parts of spirituality. He decided that he was much too young for that kind of commitment and on a much different path. With time, we grew apart, and his behavior opened doors of opportunity for me to spend more of my free time with Bruce and in church. I started praying for changes in my life, and asked God to bless me with someone who had a love for Him in which I could learn from and spiritually grow with at the same time.

Bruce was on a mission to win me over, so he didn't mind spending more time with me while I moped over Calvin. He was right there to console me during my Calvin withdrawal era. He prayed for me when I sulked, tickled me when I couldn't smile and fed me when I went days without eating a meal. The more we hung out, the more I knew that there was something truly different about him.

"Could Bruce be that man I've been praying to you about, Lord?" I would frequently ask, after spending time with him. My answer would come in time because before either of us really realized what was happening with our friendship, we were spending lots of quality time together as special friends. What I discovered was that my "prayed over" man had been in my life all that time, but I just kept overlooking him and almost gave him away.

In 1995 we officially started dating. It was then that Bruce really started to share with me his un-resting desire to know, love and serve God better. Every morning, he called to pray with me, which I thought was so awesome. I had never dated a man who was interested in making sure that my spiritual being was fed. And because of that one quality, I knew I could be happy with him for a lifetime, which is why I accepted his marriage proposal the first time he asked.

In August of 1996, we were married. We had a beautiful wedding, with lots of family, friends and associates witnessing our festive occasion. I remember everyone standing when I entered the sanctuary. "Wow! Look at all the people," I thought. Some of the guests were whispering, as I passed by and others were sobbing. Nonetheless, both caused me to have butterflies. "Are you sure you're ready to do this Kyra Williams?" I asked myself once or twice. This was something I had dreamed about for a lifetime, so I knew I'd better make sure it was what I wanted for myself. Plus, my granny always told me, ***"Marriage is a lifetime commitment, hard work and a level of dedication you really know nothing about, until, you've had the chance to live it for yourself."*** I didn't understand what she meant, but in time I would learn for myself what commitment and dedication were really about.

I remember gracefully walking down the center isle with such pride. I was so delighted about becoming Mrs. Bruce Murrell. As I stood before the church, reciting my vows, I thought, "God smiled on me today." It was one of the happiest times of my life. My fears about marriage no longer existed. They vanished rather quickly and when we turned to be introduced to our guests as Mr. and Mrs. Bruce Murrell, I knew that I had made the right decision because my stomach was at ease.

I observed so many women who adored Bruce sharing Kleenex, and I smiled in their faces with the most vindictive smirk. By no means were they pleased with me, I had just married "The Catch of the Year." The look I gave each of them didn't seem to help much, but my point was quite clear. "I'm Mrs. Bruce Murrell and all you gold digging, sack chasers lost big today. "

2

Deception Comes Quickly

During the first two years of our marriage, we were just typical newlyweds in love. Bruce and I genuinely respected each other and God truly blessed our union. Within months, our spiritual, financial and professional lives elevated to a level we never imagined possible. Some of our friends started to envy what was happening in our lives, but positive things continued to happen for us, and life would almost feel unreal to me at times.

In December of 1997, we outgrew Bruce's bachelor pad, which we initially called home. I designed our first house, which was a thirty-five hundred square foot home and we had it built in a gated community in Norman, Oklahoma on four acres of land.

Bruce applied for his first management position during the exact same time our home was being built. He was in and out of town interviewing and the responsibility of having our home built fell strictly on me. I had just been promoted to Director of International Affairs and was working on my Doctoral Degree in International Business. My new position would require more travel and longer hours during the week, but I had been mentally preparing myself for some time and was ready to juggle the challenges of family, profession and school.

Bruce's new position required just as much traveling, which caused me to be a little concerned about our professional schedules and our marriage. I wasn't in favor of being alone in our new home either. But, once I recalled how supportive he had been when I was promoted, I wanted to be supportive of him as well. I assured him that we could work through our busy schedules and asked him not to second-guess his decision to move up the corporate ladder. For some reason, I believed that we could easily make up the quality time we lost while traveling. "Are you sure you want me to accept the position?" He kept asking. He was so hesitant about accepting the job because we were still newlyweds, but I insisted that he take the job because I knew he really wanted to.

I even occasionally joked about the frequent flyer miles he would rack up for family trips at his company's expense. Stupid me, I never realized the potential damage and distance our upscale professions would have on our family. I was young, career oriented and desired to retire by forty-five, fifty at the latest. Therefore, I missed out on my opportunity to clearly assess the ultimate price my family would pay in the end.

In 1998, we moved into our new home a few weeks before Christmas and celebrated the holidays. In February of 1999, Bruce took his first two-week trip to New York. That was the longest we had ever been apart since we'd been married. Initially, it was very difficult to have this kind of distance between us. When he first started traveling, I remember calling him so much. I just had to speak with him to tell him that I was missing him dearly.

During his first few months of travel, we talked for hours daily. He generally called right after he finished with his meetings. But, the more he traveled throughout the year, the less time he spent in his hotel room after business hours and the less time he spent on the phone talking with me. His after-hour activities increased and eventually our phone bonding time dwindled and suffered tremendously.

One Thursday evening in late September I called to tell him that he was going to be a daddy. His hotel phone and cell phone rang repeatedly. I remember thinking, "Where the hell could he be? It's one o'clock in the damn morning!" All I thought was one of two thoughts; either Bruce was hurt or having an affair. Both thoughts made me restless, and I didn't get a wink of sleep that night.

He never answered his phone, nor did he bother to call home and check in before flying out the next morning. When he arrived that afternoon, he could sense that I was irritated about something. I mentioned that I called his room, and cell phone a few times throughout the morning, but he never answered. His explanation was, that the ringer wasn't working on his room phone and his battery on his cell was dead. That bullshit should have been the first red flag for me, but I loved my husband and wanted to believe him more than anything. I wanted to believe in our marriage and I hoped that our love was beyond an affair. But, I had grown suspicious of my husband and ten months of loving Bruce Anthony Murrell from a distance had taken a toll on our relationship.

One evening while eating dinner, I mentioned my concerns about the substantial distance that appeared to be growing between us. We just didn't communicate the way we once had. He had become consumed with paperwork when he was home, and most of his weekends and free time were devoted to playing basketball and dominos with his friends. He rarely tried to spend any quality time with me and always appeared distracted whenever we made love. He just wasn't fun to be around any longer, and he certainly wasn't the same man I married. His attitude was so poor the night we had our conversation that I had to ask myself, "What was happening to my perfect, little fairytale family?" "What was happening to the wonderful friendship I had established with my husband and how long would we allow the distance between us to continue before we tried to reconcile our differences?"

Along with everything else that was happening in our lives, my hormones and emotions were also raging out of control. We were expecting our first child in April of 2000 and I had already gained fifteen pounds. My nose was starting to spread all over my face, like Mr. Potato Heads, and I strongly disliked Bruce. I didn't want that kind of drama for our family. I really wanted things in our home between us to be in order before the baby was born. I wanted our daughter to add value to our marriage, not be the reason it continued to exist. I believed, more than anything that our child deserved to be raised in a home where her parents loved one another and modeled just that on a regular basis.

Things slightly improved over the next few months. Our relationship was nothing close to what we initially shared, but I tried my best to rekindle our flame. Sometimes when I grew frustrated with our situation, I simply fussed about little things because I didn't know what else to do. What my fussing actually did for us was make a bad situation worse. I became sick and occasionally depressed from all the stress I was under, and during the end of my pregnancy, I was bed ridden. I could tell that at that particular time in my pregnancy Bruce worried about my health. He claimed he didn't want me to go into premature labor, so he eventually worked on keeping the peace between us.

Our daughter, Taylor, was finally born on April 4, 2000. She came into the world fussing and kicking, with a head full of hair. She was such an adorable little lady, and the day of her birth would prove to be one of the happiest days in life for Bruce and I. He was such a proud dad. As he stood around the birthing room closely observing the medical staff, I smiled once he became tearful after watching Taylor's vitals being taken. And wouldn't you know it, as angry as I had been with Bruce throughout my pregnancy, Taylor would come here looking just like him. That was the real icing on the cake for him. He took one look at her and fell head over hills in love with our precious jewel. That would mark the day that little Taylor not only set the sun and moon in her father's eyes, but also became the real female dictator in his life.

Bruce took two months of paternity leave to help out around the house, and during this time, he did everything a new mother would do and more. I was so proud of how dedicated he was. When I observed his interaction with Taylor and the bond they were developing, I thought, "Yeah! Things are headed in a positive direction once again for our family."

In July, Bruce went back to working his tedious schedule and was traveling city-to-city like crazy. The week of our fourth anniversary, he was able to stay home with Taylor and me for a few days, but nothing exciting between us took place. The entire time he was home, he focused on everything else but me. I thought we should have spent that time doing something special, but instead he updated files, completed his annual performance report and played with the baby.

The one evening he was free, his cell phone rang about seven o'clock. Seconds later, he walked into Taylor's nursery to inform me that he was going out to watch a basketball game with a few of his friends. He grabbed a beer out of the refrigerator, snatched his keys off the counter, and kissed the baby. "Kyra, I'll be back in about two hours. I'll be with Miles, Marcus and Cedric, if you need me." I watched him walk out the front door in disbelief, while my eyes filled with tears. We had been home all day and not once did he mention doing something special with me. But, his frat brothers could call and everything ceased. "Oh, Hell No! Bruce is going to have to help me understand this one," I angrily mumbled to myself.

Bruce hadn't been gone a good hour before our home phone rang. It was Marcus, who hardly ever called the house. He never wanted to disturb me, so he always called Bruce on his cell phone directly. I couldn't wait to get off the phone, so I could call Bruce and curse him out for lying. When I called, his voice mail immediately picked up after the first ring for over two hours, which meant it had been turned off. I continued to call and thought about leaving a message, but I wanted to surprise his sorry ass, so I continued to hang up on the recording. With me being as angry as I was, it was probably best that he didn't answer his phone because he would have quickly discovered that his spiritual woman could act a damn fool when necessary.

I knew Bruce had enough time to make it to his destination, so if they were supposed to be together, I wondered why Marcus was calling the house to speak with him? That question played over in my mind for several hours. By the time he finally called, I had calmed down a little, so when I initially answered the telephone, I was slightly sane. But, it didn't last for very long. Once he gave me that same lame ass story about his battery being dead again, I lost my cool. He said he left his phone charging in the car because his battery was low, and I knew that was a lie. His cell phone had been on the charger the entire day, and I watched him unplug it from the base right before he left the house.

He continued to stick with his lie, though. I must say he was quite determined to make me believe his story, which only made me angrier.

"Bruce, you're a liar and where are you?" I yelled.
"I told you I was going out with the fellas to the sports bar."
"Well if you're at the sports bar with the fellas, why did Marcus call here looking for you about two hours ago?"

He was dumbfounded, at a complete loss for words and searching his mind for anything he thought might help his situation. I started screaming and cursing even louder at him. Hell, I was talking so fast that it was impossible for him to get in one word, so he hung up on me. I assumed that his woman must have been in close proximity and heard me going off. He obviously didn't want to ruin their mood, but actually he should have. It would have been far easier for him to deal with her at a later date than it was going to be for him to deal with me when he finally made it home.

Bruce arrived home about two in the morning. I had taken a shower and was nursing Taylor in the living room. By then I had become completely crazy. I took the baby to her nursery and walked into our bedroom to confront him. He stood in the bathroom door with this taunting look on his face, so I asked,
"Oh! So, what do you think you're doing?"
"What do you mean, what do I think I'm doing? I think…. I'm getting ready for bed. At least, that's what it looks like to me," he replied with this bold smirk on his face.

"You might be getting ready for bed, but you won't be sleeping your black ass in this house. You'd better find your way back to wherever you just came from because they'll be no rest for you up in here tonight."

He became real cocky and replied while smacking his lips and laughing,
"I'm not going anywhere tonight Kyra. You need to relax and go in the room with the baby or I will."
"You can't tell me where to go." I screamed, as I walked up on him and swung. He grabbed me and held my arms down, which was hopeless because then I started kicking him.

The fight we had that night would go down in our marital archives. It would be the beginning of my mission to pay him back for lying to me, move on with my life, or forgive him and work out our marital problems.

He became so cold towards me after that fight. I realized that slapping him wasn't a good decision on my behalf, and because of my raging fit, I was no longer one of his favorite people. But, I was prepared to deal with the consequences of my actions. After all, he forced me to become a person in our marriage that I never thought I would have to expose him to.

Bruce was simply angry with me for my behavior, so whenever he was home, we walked by each other like total strangers, and reduced our conversation to issues pertaining strictly to our daughter and a trip to Detroit that we had already planned and paid for. The closer we got to going on our vacation; the only thing I focused on was getting myself together. I could not go home in the state of mind I was in. My heart was broken, and I cried for weeks because of that incident. I felt terrible inside, and the agony of still wanting to be in love with a deceitful man who I believed wronged me, continued to control my life. I had somehow done the unthinkable and allowed Bruce to slowly steal my joy. I felt like that scorned woman I had only heard about. My Christian walk became tainted, my attitude as a wife sucked, and any desire I once possessed to be a loving, obedient wife............no longer existed.

Bruce Murrell started some real shit when he went looking for love outside our home. He had violated my trust, broken our bond and wore me down emotionally. But that never seemed to bother him, and that is why another man was able to easily spark my attention.

3

A Family Reunion

We arrived at Detroit Metro Airport on Friday, August 1, 2001. It was a beautiful, sunny day and fluffy, white clouds covered the sky like fields of cotton. Though Bruce and I were still barely speaking, he decided to still accompany me because he didn't want me to struggle with Taylor and her things. He also had a few frat brothers from college who he wanted to see, so he really wasn't obligated to hang out with me while we were there.

Before we left Oklahoma, he made plans to get with his frat, and I knew they would keep him busy. I had gotten in touch with Katrina Taylor. She was one of my best friends in Detroit who I grew up with. She was just as ghetto fabulous as ever, loved by everyone and because we were so close, Taylor was also named after her.

We made plans to meet up as soon as I arrived in the city. But I wanted to do right by Bruce, since he wasn't from Detroit and at least see to it that he found his way to the hotel. While we were at the car rental counter, I called her from my cell phone and arranged to meet up with her later that evening.

My family was also kicking off day one of our family reunion that same day, and I wanted to make sure that I spent some quality time with them. I informed Kat, which is Katrina's nickname, to run all of her errands, and meet up with me about nine-thirty at my Aunt Irene's house. Bruce and I checked into the Residence Suites in Southfield. I changed Taylor's clothing, made sure Bruce didn't need a ride, and then headed for my auntie's house.

Everyone was there when we arrived. Cousins, aunts and uncles I hadn't seen in years came falling out of the house like roaches. My Mom was so thrilled to have us home and quite anxious to see Taylor again. She held that baby the entire evening and fussed whenever she was asked to share her moment. She hadn't seen Taylor, which was her only grandchild, since she was three weeks old, so some of her selfishness was clearly understandable.

It was so good to see everyone, and as the evening went on, it was even nicer to see that we had made it through a good portion of the day without one outbreak. My family was like most urban, black families. The only time we could come together and act half sensible was at funerals or some other depressing occasion. I say "half sensible" lightly because they have been known to show their asses during funerals, at the cemetery, inside the family cars and the church fellowship hall.

Getting along for the Williams family was as impossible as an incompetent person making a perfect score on the SAT. The family bond had been in trouble for years. My great grandfather and two of his sisters experienced differences back in the early 50's which trickled down to their offspring. This was primarily why we could only be around each other for so long before some kind of foolishness jumped off.

Most of the cousins, nieces and nephews of each great-grand sibling never really experienced a meaningful relationship. And the competition amongst Aunt Brenda's daughters was quite comical to witness. Each of them was always trying to out bling one another with their jewelry, out fox each other with their furs, and out do each other with their luxury toys. My aunts, Brenda and Irene, grew tired of the family feuding, so they decided to bring our family together for a jovial occasion and planned our family's first, William's Family Reunion. I had to buy my plane ticket in advance because I wanted to make sure I witnessed for myself the act of my family coming together and behaving half civil. I didn't want anyone to tell me about it, nor did I want to watch it on a video.

Even though things usually started off well, it was a guarantee that someone was going to have a flash back about something that happened years ago. Once the "happy juice," took effect, and the buzz was set, the madness usually surfaced. I sat back in a big, plush, high backed, chair in Aunt Irene's living room waiting for the drama to begin.

While laughing with my cousin Scooter about some of our childhood mischief, I realized that I had seen everyone, except my Uncle Daniel. Uncle Daniel was always the life of the party, and I had such fond childhood memories of him. I smiled the entire time Scooter talked about him. I also wondered why he hadn't arrived yet. But, once I really started thinking about Uncle Daniel's past behavior at family functions, I thought, "It was probably a good thing that he wasn't there yet."

Uncle Daniel was the one family member everyone loved. He always walked into a family function and brought some sunshine with him. He had been a chronic alcoholic all twenty-nine years of my life. And as much as I hate to say this, he was the family drunk who always spoke the truth about the nonsense that plagued the family, which sometimes made his sisters angry. But shoot, he didn't care; he told it like it was anyway.

Uncle Daniel never maintained employment; however, he was academically brilliant. When we were kids, Scooter and I always got into trouble for teasing him about being the only family member to ever go to college and still not have a job. Heck, we were so young and silly then, we didn't even realize that you had to not only go to college, but also, graduate. When Uncle Daniel went to college, he pledged a fraternity and came home with what we called "horseshoes," branded on his chest, and though he never graduated with a Bachelors Degree, he truly mastered loving his family in spite of our shortcomings. I couldn't resist any longer, so I finally asked about him.

"Where's Uncle D?"

"He'll be here shortly," my Aunt Brenda, replied.

"Yeah, he wouldn't miss a gathering like this for nothing in the world. We got three things here that flush out drunks: food, family and LIQUOR," my cousin Roy stated with the dumbest look on his face.

I was disgusted with his comment. It was so inappropriate for the occasion. "Yeah, I'm home," I thought to myself, and then I heard the doorbell. "Saved by the bell, Roy. I was just about to get in your ass," I stated, as I got up and walked to the door.

Kat was running a few minutes late and apologized for arriving at nine forty-five. Seeing her brought back so many great memories of growing up in a big city. I was ready to leave as soon as she arrived, but my Uncle Daniel arrived just as she was walking through the door. I spent about twenty minutes clowning with him, while he tried to flirt with Kat. "Come on now Uncle D, she's twenty plus years younger than you," Scooter yelled from the living room. He was still Uncle Daniel, just as silly as ever and reeking of alcohol. I introduced him to Taylor, and while he awed over her, I waved bye to my Mom and slipped out the side door.

Kat and I walked down the driveway laughing, hugging and chatting about old times. She was all ready to show me a good time and wanted to know which of our old friends I wanted to visit first. I hadn't seen many of my friends in at least ten years, so I told her to take me to see Janet, our other partner in crime. Janet was the third of our little back-in-the-day click, which was the, S.C.P.G.'s, "Schoolcraft Playgirls." When we arrived, Janet wasn't able to visit with us long. She had to work the graveyard shift that evening and was on her way out.

It was still rather early, and I was far from ready to go back to the hotel and sit with Bruce. Kat anxiously suggested that we go to her Uncle Woody's club to have a drink. I was game for whatever. I hadn't had a drink in months, but could surely use one. I also thought it would be fun if we could toast to life and the joy of

19

friendship, so I quickly agreed to having a nightcap. Kat shifted her gear to drive, and we headed for Schoolcraft.

Schoolcraft was a major street that went from one jumping neighborhood to the next. As we drove down the Craft to Kat's uncle's club, I thought of some of my old friends, some of the silly things we use to do and what they had accomplished in life since high school. As we came up on Piedmont and passed our old middle school, I asked Kat about some of our classmates. She was still in touch with so many of them and it seemed as though she knew what was going on with everyone. She quickly updated me on every person I asked about, but for some reason, Everett Barnett was a conversation piece that stuck with us.

"Girl what is up with Everett?" I asked.
"Old Wet-Set," She replied, which was a nickname we had given him back as kids because he wore a juicy, long Jheri Curl.
"I spoke with him earlier in the week and told him that you were coming to town this weekend."
"You did? What did he say?"
"He told me that he wanted to see you and for me to buzz him up when you got here. I'm going to call him now and see if he'll come up to the bar and hang out with us tonight."

As I reflected over my past, I envisioned my middle school days and remembered Everett clearly. He was a pudgy little dude, with a juicy, whopped Jheri Curl Afro, and a big mouth. Our primary conversation as kids always consisted of me telling him to "Shut Up." Everett was the classmate who always talked too much noise, and then wanted to fight if you made him look bad by defending yourself. He always threatened the girls in our class, but I didn't care because everyone in the school and in my neighborhood knew our family. They knew the "Williams Klan," was well known for being no nonsense and deep up in Vetal Middle School.

Everett and I weren't close as kids, but I was curious to see what he had done with his life. Once we arrived at the club, Kat called him from her cell phone a second time to see if he was free for the evening. He agreed to meet up with us so we sat around conversing while we waited. At about eleven-fifty, we ordered drinks. Kat and I continued to share old stories and laughed with some guys who were trying to flirt with us at the bar.

"Girl where the hell is Everett?" I finally asked, after looking at my watch and noticing that we had been waiting for almost an hour.
"Everett's still jive as hell, Kyra. You want me to call him again?"
"Nope, I sure don't. If he doesn't come within the next ten minutes, we can blow this joint and holla at him later."

Within seconds of me making my statement, I turned to look at security as they searched males entering the club. There stood this golden, semi-tall, hella fine cutie with a blue, bent brim, ball cap on. His cap slightly covered his eyes, and his smile was one for a Kodak moment. I had not seen Everett in years, but this fella's facial features slightly favored the Everett I remembered from middle school. My mouth began to water, as I tapped Kat and asked, "Girl is that Everett?"

Before she could even respond, I cut her off and stated, "Damn that boy done got FINE AS HELL." As he approached us, I stared at him, while licking my lips a few times. I thought to myself "What a treat, WHAT A TREAT!" He had on this Roca Wear jean outfit that gave him a slight ruff neck look, which immediately turned me on. Not to mention how his distinctive walk had Kat and I both lusting, as we checked him out from head to toe.

His look was much different from Bruce's Corporate America look, which I was so used to seeing and had grown completely bored with. His face was well manicured. I mean, his low cut beard and mustache were trimmed and edged to perfection. He was flawless, and his lips had this soft spongy look. Awe, his lips, um, they were actually a little wet from where he had moistened them right as he made it to our seats. His seductive hazel eyes said

21

something to me only a woman could interpret. All I could think while gazing into them was, "Thank God I am a woman," because they were truly communicating with me, and I loved every bit of what they were saying.

I smiled when he put his hand on my chair. I just kept thinking about how fine he had become with age. He was truly a sex symbol and ladies all over the club paused to check him out when he walked through the bar that night.

"What's up ladies?" He asked, after we passed the wordless flirting stage.

"Nothing much," Kat and I replied in sync, as we pinched each other's arm inconspicuously. His smile was so gorgeous that any woman in her right frame of mind would love to freeze-frame it and put it on display for daily inspiration. When I stood up to hug him, I tried to down play his sex appeal. However, the woman in me wouldn't allow me to suppress my thoughts any longer. "Damn Everett, you've gotten fine with age, haven't you?" I blurted out.

Though he tried to remain modest, all he could do was smile from ear to ear because the brotha knew it was true. He had it goin on and his ego was larger than life from all of the compliments. He tried not to respond to my comment, but he began blushing big time. To avoid appearing arrogant, he simply thanked me and then inquired about what I had been doing with my life over the years. After sharing my accomplishments, he shared with me that he had two teenage daughters, had been working for General Motors for ten years and in his spare time; he bought, refurbished and rented out homes.

We engaged in small talk for as long as we could, but it was difficult for me to remain focused, so our small talk ended rather quickly. I noticed that he was checking me out, and I could feel the vibes brewing between us. I tried to redirect his attraction for me towards Kat a few times, but it was very obvious that his interest was without a doubt in me. He touched my ring on my left finger a few times. I believe, to inquire about my marital status without directly asking. But, I never confirmed one way or the other. If he really wanted to know bad enough, he was going to have to ask. I wasn't sharing any detailed information about my personal life.

While we sat around the bar talking, R. Kelly's, slow jam, "Honey Love" came on. Everett grabbed my hand, which I felt like pulling back because I was in touch with my feminine side. He led me to the dance floor, and I was lusting the entire time he was in my presence. "What ifs" started popping up in my mind like crazy? "For Real!" I thought to myself. "This brotha would snatch me up on the first slow jam for a dance." He obviously didn't know that I was still in some ways that raw, little tuff chick he grew up with. If I felt anything poking me, just one time, his fine behind was getting flipped on the dance floor for being too close and turning a sista on.

I don't even remember hearing any of the words to the song while we danced. All I know is that I was quite focused on keeping adequate space between us. I laughed at him most of the time we danced because he was trying so hard to get with me. He was blunt and wasted no time trying to get re-acquainted.

"Kyra you are so beautiful."
"Why, thank you Everett. I didn't think you noticed."
"So, are you married?" He asked.
"See, why is he all in my business?" I thought to myself before answering his question with a quick, sassy, "Yes."

I knew he might not try to pursue me after my reply, but I hoped that he would at least continue to ask about things happening in my life. I realized that I was totally out of line for wanting him to, but I didn't care.

"You said, "Yes," you're married Kyra?"
"Yes! I sure did."
"Well where the hell is your husband and why did he let you come out by yourself?"

"Bruce went out with some of his frat brothers."

"You mean to tell me that your husband intentionally let you come out alone in the D tonight?"

"He sure did! My husband knows what he has in me, and he knows he can trust me."

"Yeah! But he can't trust me, or brotha's like me."

I don't know where our conversation was headed, but the DJ rescued us both. He put on a fast song that disturbed our groove and just as fast as we walked to the dance floor to slow dance, we walked off to get back to Kat and our drinks. Realistically, fast dancing is far from what Everett had in mind for me that night. He wanted to be close to me, or at least close enough to smell my perfume. He wanted to feel my curves, pry into my married life and see where my head was.

Actually, I was relieved when we finally walked off the dance floor. I was growing weak to his twenty questions. Plus, he smelled hella good. To be perfectly honest, had I spent another minute on that dance floor with him, I might have said or done something I was going to regret for the remainder of my visit.

While walking back to our seats, I had to thoroughly check him out one additional time. I noticed some qualities that I had missed when he initially entered the club. My thoughts were far from focused, as I walked behind him admiring everything about him. I adored this man from head to toe, and his Bvlgari cologne was calling my name. It had me so distracted that I stopped in mid-stride and suggested that we take some photos because I needed to be close to him once more.

Kat was looking over at us from the bar smiling. I motioned for her to come over to the corner where the photo backdrop was hanging and take a picture with us. I wasn't stupid. I knew that I couldn't take a photo of just me and another man home. But this night with Mr. Everett Barnett, I wanted to remember for a lifetime. I pulled my money out of my purse to pay for our photo, and

Everett insisted that I allow him to cover the tab. I felt like I should have paid since it had been my suggestion for us to take the picture to begin with. But he wasn't feeling me and refused my offer.

Once we were back at our seats, we ordered one last drink. I repeatedly thanked Everett for his hospitality. We partied a little longer, and finally our good time in the club, unfortunately, came to an end. Everett wasn't quite ready for the night to end, so he suggested that we allow him to take us to Mildred's for breakfast. I was a mommy and a wife on a self-inflicted curfew and thought it was best to ask him for a rain check. I sipped down the last of my wine, grabbed my purse and he walked us to the car.

He smiled the entire time we were walking and talked major noise to me about going in so early. I gave him a hard time in return, and again commented on his sex appeal and that beautiful toothpaste commercial smile of his that managed to keep my attention all night long. Smiling from ear to ear, he let out this cute little laugh, while opening the car door. He wrote his number on a piece of paper for me, and I gave him my business card with my personal numbers on the back.

"Damn! I rate the business card," he sarcastically replied, while softly shutting my door.

"I wrote my personal numbers on the back, silly."

"You're lucky; I was about to tell you to give me my scratch paper back," he stated while walking away.

Once Everett was far enough away from the car, Kat and I gave each other repeated high fives as we watched him climb into his metallic blue Escalade.

"Girl, if you don't get with that man, you're a fool," I screamed, while giving Kat five an additional time.

To be perfectly honest, I never gave us much consideration, though Kat and I talked about him all the way to my Aunt Irene's house. Yeah, I wasn't really happy with Bruce, but I wasn't really sure about cheating on him for revenge either.

I didn't see Everett for the remainder of my visit home, but I certainly thought about him. I thought about his eyes, his lips, his smile and how great he made me feel that Friday night. I couldn't even begin to count on my hands and feet the number of times I felt tempted to call and say "Hello." I tried to remind myself that I was a woman with integrity, so I tried to stay focused on spending quality time with my family.

When it was time to return to Oklahoma, I hoped that I would wrap up my trip with lots of fond memories of my first family reunion. I also wanted to leave my superficial desires to see Everett once again behind. When I boarded my plane, Everett seemed to be all I could think about and adoring thoughts of him were embedded deep within my mind. Because he was so much fun, complimenting when it came to me and fine as ever, thoughts of him taunted the hell out of me my entire flight home.

4

Revived By The Past

Once I returned home, I tried to put my trip and thoughts of Mr. Barnett behind me. I went on with my day-to-day living, which was full of depression, loneliness, anger and tears. I was miserable with my current situation, starving for any kind of affection and ready to just lose my mind. Bruce was back to traveling with his job, and we were basically still only talking to each other about topics pertaining to Taylor. The only difference now was that we argued about issues dealing with her and could barely stand being in each other's presence. I wasn't getting anything from him resembling companionship and found myself spiritually sinking to an unspeakable low. I kept thinking to myself. "If I only had a special friend I could confide in or if I only had an innocent friendship, things would be a little better for me."

One day while driving home, Everett's smile came to mind as clear as if he were standing right in my very presence. I thought about him for a minute then pulled out my organizer. I searched for his cell phone number, which was still on the piece of paper he had originally given me that night. I hesitantly dialed his number, and once the phone started ringing, I relaxed.

I initially planned to strike up a superficial conversation when he answered the phone. Hell, I couldn't say, "All I've been thinking about since I left Detroit is your fine butt and that smile of yours." So, when he answered his phone, I said, "Oh! What, a black woman can't get a call from any of her sorry so-called homies in the D?" He laughed and from there, the conversation blossomed. We chatted briefly, but our conversation was full of substance. When I hung up the phone with him, I felt like a rejuvenated woman. I smiled to myself and thought, "Man, I should." However, before I could go any further with that thought, my conscience kicked in and reminded me that I possessed concrete morals, which shouldn't be compromised.

I allowed weeks to pass without calling, but thoughts of Everett frequently came to mind. I just wasn't ready to be a cheater, so I concluded for the sake of maintaining my dignity, that I would not pursue anything other than a friendship with him, and went about with my daily routine.

In late August of 2001, while sitting in my office, my direct line rang. "International Affairs, Kyra Murrell speaking. How may I help you?" "Kyra, I've been thinking about you." A gentleman stated, in a sexy, mouth-watering tone. I was totally caught off guard. I thought one of my co-workers was playing on the phone. We teased each other in the office like that sometimes, so my response was quite unprofessional. "Who is this?" I asked. "Your ex lover." He replied. But, I knew my ex's voice quite well after spending so many years of my life with him. I clearly did not recognize the voice of the person on my phone, so I abruptly stated, "Stop playing on the phone or get hung the hell up on." Right then, he went into a belly laugh. "Hey lil. girl, you're still mean. It's me, Everett."

My mouth flew wide open. My hands became clammy and butterflies accumulated in my stomach right after he said his name.

"Everett," I repeated, as my mind quickly processed our last conversation, which had been over two weeks ago. Memories of our very special reunion at Woody's earlier that month suddenly re-played in my mind. Without wasting time I said, "Everett! Boy you're so crazy. I almost hung up on you."

I was simply trippin about him being on the phone. But what really threw me was that he initiated the call.

"What is it that I could have possibly said or done during our last conversation for me to rate a call today?" I asked.

"Well Ms. Lady, it was such a beautiful day and you came to mind. After thinking about you for so long, I remembered that I had your business card in my wallet, so I thought I would call you at work and surprise you."

"Well I feel honored that a beautiful sunny day brought thoughts of me to mind."

"I'm going to stop beating around the bush. I called because I really want to see you again Kyra. I've been thinking about you since you left."

"What!!!!!!!!! What did you say?"

"I've been thinking about you since I left the club that night. You've been in my dreams; the first thought on my mind each morning and your smile accompanies me to work daily. I've missed you since we last talked a few weeks ago, and I want to see you again."

That was so unexpected. Once his comment registered, my chin hit my chest and quickly bounced back into a big Kool-Aide smile.

"Where did that come from," I thought to myself, as I felt my jaws tightening and my face hurting from smiling so hard. He continued with his conversation, and my heart started pounding so hard that I could actually hear it beating. "Let me fly you to Detroit for a visit." My eyes immediately bucked open, as I tried to convince myself that this conversation with Everett wasn't really happening.

I tried to remember all of those morals my conscience reminded me about the last time I spoke with him. Fortunately, this time for Bruce's sake, I remembered and replied correctly. "I can't come there to see you Everett, I'm a married woman." Not that it really mattered, but I was trying to do the right thing. Nonetheless, I still wanted him to make it a challenge for me to stick with my "NO." If he got the nerve to ask a second time, I was going to see how serious he was and suggest that he come to Oklahoma to visit me instead. With as much as I thought about him after I left Detroit, I knew it would be nice to see him again.

I was sure that if he came to see me in Oklahoma, I could control the situation between us better. Shortly after rejecting his first request, he finally asked the big question once again, and again, I rejected his offer. Good thing he wasn't accepting "no" for an answer. Finally he asked, "Well Kyra, can I come to Oklahoma and visit you?"

My back was up against the wall now. After his question, I really became speechless. I tried to keep that cool, calm, collective attitude I had been portraying since we reunited, so I nonchalantly replied, "I'll think about it."

"Well, just let me know when and if you decide you want some company."

"Sure Everett, I'll think about it and let you know what I come up with. But, I know you're not going to seriously leave Detroit and come all this way to visit me."

"Kyra, I can show you better than I can tell you. Just let me know what your schedule is looking like, and I'll be there."

I remembered that Bruce applied for a new administration position with his corporate office a few months earlier. If he accepted the position, he would have to leave town for a few weeks. I told Everett I would consider a visit and let him know something real soon. "Kyra, make sure you don't keep me waiting too long. I'm very serious about coming, and I really do want to see you again."

We said our short goodbyes, and he hung up the phone. I held the receiver in my hand for about fifty seconds reflecting over our conversation before actually hanging it up. When I finally put the receiver on the hook, I smiled for the longest time. I wondered if he were doing the same on his end and if he was feeling as refreshed as I did after our conversation?

I slung my chair away from my desk, sprung up from my seat like a new woman and went out into the primary working station of

30

my office. I hummed as I walked to the water cooler; I had a new song for sure ·on my mind. I bounced about the office for the remainder of the day so energized, my Administrative Assistant asked if I had hit the power ball lottery or something. Everyone seemed to notice how cheerful I had become after getting a call that day. Had they known that I had just spoken with a gentleman who made me feel like a power ball lottery winner, they might have encouraged me to speak with him more often. Because, not only had I been moody at home, but at work as well, and my employees had been catching hell ever since Bruce and I fell out.

Though Everett was not a monetary prize, it felt like I had just hit some kind of jackpot. I thought about him daily after our conversation. I often wondered what he was doing, how his day was going, and most of all, if he, himself, had some kind of significant other in his life? For some reason, I never asked him if he had a mate. I guess I was trying to prevent my curiosities about him from getting the best of me. Knowing his status early on might have significantly changed things between us, so I never asked. We continued to have a few brief-touch-and-go conversations throughout the month of September. I tried to keep my distance because I was well aware of how he made me feel and I was afraid that I might act upon it.

October arrived, and I was still having problems with Bruce. Everett and I started to talk a little more frequently, which lead to me eventually sharing some of my personal heartaches with him. Things didn't look or feel like they were going to ever get better with Bruce and I. I was struggling with the thought of not leaving him because I had been raised in a single parent home. I desperately wanted Taylor to be raised by both of her parents. I always felt like I missed out on the real experience of having my biological father in the home, and I wanted something better for my child. As a child, I always wanted to know the man who contributed to my existence. After observing Bruce with Taylor, I realized that I missed out on my father teaching me the things a father teaches his daughter about life and men. And though I survived his absence and had been successful in life as well, it never changed the fact that I always felt like I missed out on the opportunity to experience the true beauty of a father's love.

I kept asking Bruce, "What do you suggest we do about our marriage?" He never had an answer. I suggested that we try marital counseling. But he never responded with anything that could make our situation better and that was confirmation enough for me. His actions around the house, clearly spelled out, "Affair." He was isolated, coldhearted, very short when it came to patience with me, always looking for any small reason to leave the house and devoted one hundred percent of his free time to Taylor. I had finally grown physically tired of our situation and mentally pathetic. I was tired of feeling lonely, depressed and stressed out, and I was ready for some changes to occur in my life.

My ability to resist Everett's request to visit had become weak. My constant problems at home had taken a toll on me and made me even more anxious to see him. As a matter a fact, the unhappier I became with my situation at home, the more I longed to see him. The more I longed to see him, the more I knew having an affair could become a reality.

One Saturday morning, after Bruce left the house to attend his monthly fraternity meeting, I was sitting around thinking about where life was taking me. Everything about my life, at the present time, appeared to be one big blur for me. The one thing that appeared to keep me going was my yearning to see Everett again. I sat on the living room couch with my legs curled up under me, repeatedly thinking about how Bruce had been treating me. I thought about the big argument we had before we went to Detroit and the limited amount of time he had been spending at home. I felt powerless, betrayed and bitter as hell. I didn't feel like suppressing my desires to see Everett any longer, so "Fuck it!" I uttered to myself that morning, snatched up the phone receiver and dialed his number.

"Hello." He swiftly answered.

"Dang! The phone didn't even ring, did it?"

"Sure it did. What are you doing calling me so early? Where's Bruce?"

"He went to a fraternity meeting. When he gets together with his frat, it's usually an all day event. They'll probably go out hoochie hopping afterwards, so I don't expect him home til late tonight."

He laughed, which was what I needed to relax and proceed with our conversation. I tried to find the courage to extend him an invitation. When I found it, I said,

"Hey Everett, I was thinking about you this morning and thought I would call you and invite you to accompany me on a trip to Florida with a few of my friends from work."

"You and your friends?" He repeated.

"Yeah! You could meet me there and pretend to be my cousin and no one would suspect a thing."

"Yeah, right, no one would suspect anything. Girl I'd be all over you like a cheap ass Value Village suit. Everyone would know that I was far more than just your cousin."

I sucked my tongue, while sighing and asked,

"So are you going to come or not?"

"Hell Yeah, I'm coming. When do you want me there? Shit, I'll pack my bags, be there first thing tomorrow and sleep in your garage until it's time to leave."

"Like hell you will." I quickly replied.

"I would if you wanted me to."

"Are you coming or not Everett?"

He accepted my invitation because he, too, was very anxious to see me again. He was more excited about getting to play the role of my cousin and sarcastically replied,

"Baby, I can play the cousin role well."

"We'll let me be the judge of that for myself."

33

"Are we going to be kissing cousins, too, Kyra? Because I know one thing for sure, I'm not coming all that way to give you dap all damn weekend."

I laughed at his comment and even felt slightly revitalized from just hearing his voice. For the first time in weeks, I could see a dim light at the end of my tunnel of life. Even though it was a major violation of my wedding vows, it was really good to feel hopeful about something. I told Everett, I would get back with him on flight information after I looked it up on the Internet. But, I began to get cold feet after a few days, so I called him back and canceled. I told him I couldn't find any reasonable ticket rates and would try again in the near future. I don't believe that he really trusted my reason for canceling, and I could tell by his tone that he was slightly disappointed. He assured me that he wasn't mad, and expressed that he would, in fact, be available for a visit anytime. He also guaranteed me that there would be nothing I could say or do the next time that would detour him from visiting. Before hanging up with me that day, he made it quite clear that I better not ask him to visit in the future, if I really wasn't ready.

The festivities in Florida with my girlfriends from work came and went as planned. Though I thought about Everett that entire weekend, I was sure that I had made the right decision by waiting to see him. I hoped that time would eventually allow us the opportunity to get together. I just didn't want to rush things between him and I, due to my unhappiness.

Weekly phone conversations between us continued. I loved talking to this man, and my desires to see him were growing out of control. My feelings were intensifying quickly, and I was growing quite attached to him. I finally got to a point in my life where I had to see him. If I didn't act on my impulses soon, I was going to either have a nervous break down from trying to endure Bruce or go completely nuts from my yearning to be held by Everett.

After Bruce returned from his interview, he informed me that he had accepted the upper administration position in his corporate office. He would have to leave home in a month and would be gone for seven to ten weeks of training. "Perfect," I whispered to myself, as he shared the details of his trip. The big break I had been waiting for had finally arrived. "I have to let Everett know," I thought, the entire time Bruce was talking. That evening, I was extremely restless. I tossed and turned and watched the clock until I couldn't watch it any longer.

At five fifty the next morning, I got out of bed early and prepared for work. As I gathered my things to head out, I observed Bruce out of the corner of my eye. He was quite chipper and bounced through the house like an impotent dick that had just been introduced to Viagra for the first time. I shook my head in disgust and rolled my eyes at him. I felt absolutely no guilt or reservation about my decision to call Everett. I grabbed Taylor, my purse and headed out the door. Once I pulled out of the driveway, I immediately reached for my cell phone and called Everett to inform him of the news. He was thrilled and guaranteed me that he was going to purchase his ticket by noon that same day to prevent me from changing my mind once again.

With him purchasing his ticket thirty days in advance, it really seemed like an extremely long time until our visit. As time ticked on, some days appeared to drag on longer than others. We both found ourselves counting down the remaining days until our rendezvous. I must admit that the last fourteen days in the month of October felt like years to me because they came and went so slowly.

There were days when we talked on the phone two, three and sometimes four times a day. We were clearly trying to bond before the big visit. Due to our intense communication, I developed a real interest in him and what I initially learned from our conversations was that he possessed several characteristics that were appealing to me. He was intelligent, provided me with great conversation and had an awesome sense of humor. He said lots of cute, little mushy things that made me feel young again and just as silly as ever. But most of all, he was everything I missed and needed in a companion, and that's what made it most difficult to divert my interest in him.

Everett had me in touch with emotions I hadn't explored in years. Actually, I almost forgot they even existed, until he encouraged me to use them once again. One of the things I enjoyed most about him was this "Daily-Count-Down-Till-Kyra," craze he did every time we were about to hang up. This was one of his cutest, little gestures, and I loved it. "Ok.... Kyra, I have ten days, five hours, ten minutes and fifty-two seconds left until I see you." Wow! I got so tickled. My heart always felt like warm, mushy butter after hearing him say that. As a matter of fact, every time I spoke with him, I hung up the phone feeling like a dizzy, little high school girl in love with a sports jock. But, what was most heartbreaking about this entire situation with Everett was that Bruce once made me feel that exact same way.

I often wondered, "What was going to become of this thing I was venturing into with a man over twelve hundred miles away from me and how would I maintain my emotions as a married woman?" I rarely had any answers for the questions I often thought about. At times, I tried not to ponder on them too much, but some days they were so intense that there was no way to avoid them.

I figured since I was this big time, degreed, professional sista, I would be able to keep this situation in the right perspective. But, with the way he was romancing my intellect and feeding my emotionally starved needs, I would quickly discover that it wasn't going to be as easy as I thought to restrain myself. I also discovered that when it comes to relationships or emotions, neither college degrees, nor one's professional status, regulates a damn thing when the heart is involved.

5

Mr. B's Visit to OKC

The singer, Tyrese, had just released his new song, "What Am I Gonna Do." This song was climbing the charts right when our relationship was blossoming. I could relate considering I had Everett-on-the-brain like crazy. "Shit, what am I getting into now," I thought a time or two to myself because I realized that I might be getting in over my head. I knew that I should totally leave that situation alone, but the desire to commit adultery had gotten the best of me.

The week of Everett's trip finally arrived. I remember wanting to do something different and tremendously special, so I called him that Monday evening and asked, "If I were a Genie and I could grant two realistic wishes, what would you wish for?" I could tell that he was completely surprised and caught off guard by my question. When he attempted to respond, the shock from my question was clearly heard in his voice. Instead of answering my question immediately, he stated that he needed time to think about a response. I understood his position. I couldn't imagine anyone wanting to rush and provide an answer to such an unusual question? But, I was very anxious to hear his response and more anxious to make it a reality.

Thursday morning, I sprung out of bed like I was on some kind of drug. Everett would be in my presence in a few hours, and I was thrilled about us spending the weekend together. While I got dressed for work, I moved about the house preparing a mental agenda for his visit. I poured a glass of juice and grabbed my things. Just as I was heading out of the door, the phone rang and it was Bruce. "Damn, what does he want?" Bruce was notorious for calling early to mess up my day. I knew if I didn't answer the phone, he would call my cell phone and my job, if necessary, until he reached me, so I answered.

"Hello."

"Good morning, Kyra."

"Hey Bruce."

"Where's the baby?"

"She's right here, would you like to speak with her?"

"No, I have to get down to my meeting. I was just calling the two of you to say good morning."

"Oh! Ok. Well good morning," I coldly replied.
Suddenly, there was ten seconds of silence on his end. I had reversed the outcome on him and managed to mess up his day instead.

"Drive carefully and I'll call you and the baby later," he replied. I didn't bother wasting my time with a response. I just rolled my eyes way up in my head, and hung up the phone.

I was nervous at work all that day. I remember looking at my office clock and it being twelve o'clock noon. I hadn't been very productive due to my anxiousness, so I decided to leave work a little early. I grabbed some outgoing mail off my desk, tossed it in my assistant's mailbox, and walked to the elevator. While walking to my car, I received a call from Everett. He called to inform me that he was at the Detroit Metro Airport waiting to board his plane.

"Ok baby, I'll see you when you get here. Have a safe flight."

"I can't wait to see you," he stated.

"Me either." I replied and then the phone went dead.

I almost became distracted with thoughts of doubt about his trip, but I knew it was too late for regrets, and turning back wasn't an option. I tried to take some deep cleansing breaths to relax, which wasn't working at first. But, once I allowed myself to truly relax, I felt calm enough to go on with my plans.

While driving to Penn Square Mall, I thought about one of my past conversations with Everett. I remembered him sharing with me that Mountain Dew was one of his favorite drinks, so I made sure I picked up a bottle for him. I was going to chill it on ice and would have it waiting in the cup holder of my Jag when he arrived. I also got some cards and freshly cut, long stemmed roses. During his visit, it was my intention to give him a card every morning. If I was going to leave a lasting impression, each one had to say just the right thing.

Once I made it home, I sat at the desk in my office and wrote special thoughts in each card. These were thoughts that I found myself pondering over days before his visit. I would give him his first card entitled, "Thanks" the night he arrived. Each card would include ten personal thoughts that would specifically express what I was thankful to him for. On Friday morning he would wake up to a second card entitled, "You," and the last two cards would be entitled, "So and Much." Giving him a card a day would be my very own unique way of saying **Thank You So Much** for his friendship.

I glanced over the material written in each card one last time to check for errors. "Kyra, girl you've done it again," I said to myself, as I admired my creativity. I was so caught up in the moment, when I looked over at the clock; I realized that it was almost time to leave for the airport. I quickly called Bruce's sister to talk to Taylor, but she was already asleep.

I rushed to the bathroom, showered, put on one of the sexiest bra and panty sets I owned, powdered my face and threw on a two-piece suit that made a statement all by itself. Snoop Dog's song "Wrong Idea" came on the radio, and was playing in the background while I was getting dressed. I caught myself behaving like a kid, which I loved. I hadn't felt that silly in years. I danced from my closet to my bathroom sink, like a rap video girl, bouncing and shaking like a fool. I laughed at myself a few times; when I considered the way I was shaking my ass. I thought my performance would have been a hell of a treat for some lucky guy, but that thought was interrupted, as I caught a glimpse of the clock and realized that time had quickly diminished.

I scrambled through my shoes to find the right pair and slid them on, while walking out of the room. I stopped once I made it to the full-length mirror on my door, took one last look at myself and gave my reflection two thumbs up. "Yeah Ky, you're looking good tonight," I said to myself, while grabbing my keys and three slow jam CD's off my kitchen counter. I set the house alarm, jumped in my car and headed for the airport.

I arrived about fifteen minutes early, allowing myself just enough time to park and walk inside. Due to the September 11th terrorist attack, no one could walk pass the military checkpoint leading to the arrival gates. Everything about the environment in Will Roger's World Airport appeared very gloomy. People waiting for travelers weren't as chipper as usual, and I got the eeriest feeling as I observed the expressions on many of the arriving travelers' faces.

I sat on a window ledge, which allowed me to look down the terminal and anxiously watched for Everett. Finally, travelers started coming up the terminal in packs after about twenty minutes of waiting. People standing around with me began to meet up with their parties and there I was still waiting thirty minutes later. I started to question myself as to where Everett was or if he had missed his connecting flight. Actually, what I started thinking was every kind of crazy thought a nervous person might consider when tipping out on their mate for the very first time.

I was ready to get out of the public setting before someone I knew saw me and was later telling my business. Just as I started to move from my location to check the flight monitors, I noticed this attractive guy, with this distinctive walk, walking up the terminal. Surely, this guy couldn't be my Everett because my Everett was stylish and this guy had on work clothes. "A brother from Detroit would certainly know better than traveling all this way to meet a classy white-collar diva like myself in blue-collar work attire," I thought. I had big dinner plans for us that night, and if this guy was my Everett, we were certainly not going straight to dinner from the airport, as I originally planned.

The closer this guy got to me, the more he looked like Everett, and sure enough, it was, in fact, him. When he finally made it to the end of the terminal, I just smiled, and forgot all about the little uppity nonsense going on in my mind. "Hey baby," he stated, while approaching me with the biggest smile on his face. He wrapped his arms around me, gave me an innocent smooch on the cheek and a firm hug. What was a woman to do; the brotha was still fine in his work clothes, and he still made me feel good all over.

"You know you have some real guts traveling this far in work clothes to see a sista. You knew I was going to be looking scrumptious tonight, so what's up with you and that gear of yours?" He jokingly frowned and replied, "Yeah, I know better, I should have changed, but you should know by now that it's not just about the attire, it's about the quality of the man." I knew he was right. I couldn't argue with facts, so I pointed in the direction of baggage claim, and we headed that way.

We couldn't walk hand-in-hand, while walking to get his luggage, so we walked as close to each other as we possibly could without giving ourselves away. The conveyer belt started moving just as we arrived on the lower level. We watched black pulley bags go around a million times before he finally noticed his. Once he retrieved his bags, we headed to the parking garage. My car was parked rather far out, but because of the company, I didn't mind the extremely long walk at all.

When we made it to the car, there in the passenger seat sat his first card (Thanks), along with a single long stemmed rose. To me, that rose symbolized the everlasting torch of friendship I hoped to establish with him more than anything in the world. In the cup holder sat his bottle of chilled Mountain Dew, which he immediately grabbed after closing his door. I slid my little sexy self in the car, shut my door and looked over at him. With the biggest smile on my face I mentioned that I had made reservations for dinner at Marc Anthony's. He said that he was a little hungry, but wanted to shower and get out of his "Monkey suit," first. I was certainly glad to hear him say that because the restaurant was a luxurious dining facility in Nicholas Hills, and his appearance wasn't at all fitting for the occasion.

He looked me up and down and grinned from ear to ear, as I pulled up to the cashier's window to pay for parking. I knew I was looking spectacular, but didn't want to come off too cocky. I just ignored his behavior to appear modest and rolled down my window.

"That will be two dollars," the cashier stated. I reached into my back seat and grabbed my oversized, burnt orange, Coach purse. I dug around in it for a few seconds to find my wallet, but I was having little success. Everett looked at me with the silliest expression on his face for a few seconds. "Here let me pay," he stated, while holding a five-dollar bill in his hand. "No way, man; you are my guest, and I'll cover the bill."

I could tell that my comment threw him off a little, because expressions don't lie. The expression on his face suggested to me that he was not used to a woman who flaunted her self-sufficient qualities. I pushed his money away replying, "Everett, all classy women know the importance of paying our own way sometimes without compromising our man's manhood. Thank you for the offer, but as I said before, I'm paying for the parking."

I was so thrilled about him being in Oklahoma City, I seemed to almost instantly experience problems with controlling my feelings, which always seemed to overpower me. The song, "What Am I Gonna Do," by Tyrese came on shortly after we pulled away from the cashier's window and set the mood from there. I looked over at Everett with slightly glazed eyes and felt compelled to share my thoughts.

"Everett, every time I hear this song, I immediately think about you. I listen to the words, and they always generate pleasant thoughts of you."

"Oh, is that right," he asked, while giving me direct eye contact with those bedroom eyes of his.

"That's right, Mr. Man," I repeated.

As he intensely listened to the song, it was evident that he was feeling Tyrese to some degree. It was at that very moment that I realized just how in touch he was with his feminine side. His ability to expose his sensitive side did not cause him to negotiate his masculinity to me one bit. It felt good to observe him, as he enjoyed the lyrics of the song in the same manner in which I did. Most men I encountered in the past could only appreciate a beat, but here Mr. Barnett was appreciating the words.

I thought about the inquiry I made earlier to him about a Genie and granting wishes. He had never given me an answer, and I was still quite curious to know if he would come up with something unique.

"Everett, have you decided what you would like to request with your two wishes?" I asked while smiling because I knew he had something creative in mind.

"Yes. My first wish is for us to have a nice time together this weekend. My second is to see you again real soon."

After an answer like that, my facial expression completely changed. My smile went away, the heavy pounding of my heart relaxed, and I thought to myself, "DAMN! Is that all? What a way to waste some wishes. We're going to have a good time, and we're going to see each other again. Why in the world would he wish for something that required no real work at all?"

I had to ask him if he was sure that he wanted to use his wishes on something that was certain to happen for us. When he replied,

"Yes." I knew that this was in fact the way he wanted to use his wishes, and I left the issue alone.

6

Busy Hands

The remainder of the trip to my house was in silence. As I pulled into the driveway, butterflies gathered in my stomach. I knew I shouldn't bring another man into the house I shared with my husband. But since my husband wasn't acting like much of a husband, I tried to immediately end the guilt that was trying to damper my evening. I entered the house with caution, as I thought of Bruce coming home for the weekend to surprise me. However, reality quickly kicked in and I immediately recognized that my thought was nothing more than a fantasy.

We put his luggage in the guest room, and I gave him a tour of the house. Once we completed his tour, it amazed us both that we ended up at the bathroom door. "I guess this means you need a bath." I mumbled, as I pulled a towel and bath cloth out of the closet. Then I handed him a fresh bar of soap. When I walked into the den, I could hear the water from the shower pounding against the tub. I expected him to come out and ask for something, and when he didn't, I knew he wouldn't be very long.

After many reminders from a hungry stomach and thirty minutes of waiting, I had become sleepy. But when Everett finally walked into the den, "Damn! Damn! DAMN!" was all I could say. That brotha had thrown on a nice casual outfit; some smell good and looked BEAUTIFUL. "Now that's the Everett I remembered seeing in August," I thought, as I briefly stared him up and down. He was too fine, with those gorgeous eyes of his. He had the kind of sex appeal that simply stood out. In fact, that's one of the main reasons I couldn't get him off my mind after I left Detroit.

We sat around talking about his flight and the itinerary I had pulled together for the weekend. We actually chatted for so long that time seemed to get away from us and we missed our reservation. I was starving, my stomach started growling, and I still needed something to eat. Finally, loud grumbling interrupted the discussion we were having.

"I see someone is hungry," Everett stated, while putting on his shoes

"Yeah I am, but with it being so late, I don't want much to eat. You know a woman can't keep her girlish figure by eating late and going to bed on a heavy meal."

"So, is that how you have held on to that school girl figure of yours?"

Because I was flattered and trying not to show it too much, I did this stupid, little, modest chick snicker I do sometimes. There was just no way around it though, and we both burst out laughing.

"Kyra, you know you're fine, with your sexy, beautiful self." Everett stated, while walking up on me. I knew it was time to get out of the house alone with him because he was about to be too close for comfort.

"Come on nut, we need to get something to eat," I said.

"Yeah we better before I get to snacking on you." He sarcastically replied.

"Yeah and you'll get bit the heck back."

I grabbed my keys and suggested that we pick up our discussion in the car. As we drove around, we noticed that many of the fast food restaurants had already closed. It was after one-thirty in the morning and Oklahoma City was like a ghost town. There wasn't much to choose from, so we stopped and ordered Taco's.

"That will be seven dollars and thirty-five cents," the cashier stated. Again, Everett tried to pull out his money and pay the bill. "Put your money up; I got this," I stated. He looked at me and simply shook his head. I handed him his drink and the bag of food, which he sat between his legs to free up his hands. He tried to hold my hand, as we headed back to the house, but I drove with my left hand and held my drink in the other to prevent that from happening.

When we arrived back at the house, we sat on the floor in the den and ate. Everett sat right next to me, and I was nervous the entire time. Actually, he sat so close to me, at times, I would have sworn that he saw my thoughts long before I ever shared them. He stared at me a lot that evening and couldn't keep his hands or comments to himself. He rubbed my hands, played with my fingernails and continuously mentioned how he admired the curves of my lips. I was so busy enjoying the great laughs we were having with each other that I clearly missed the true significance of his luscious lips comment. I was totally caught off guard when he leaned over and passionately kissed me. I tried to say something to distract him, but before I could get out one word, he leaned right back in and kissed me a second time.

I really didn't know how to respond to him after that kiss. He tried to encourage me to relax and just allow things to flow naturally. But, that was impossible for me to do because passionate kissing wasn't a part of my preplanned agenda, so every time he got a little closer to me, I jumped. He rubbed my back and with each stroke, my feminine juices kicked in more and more. His touch was warm, soothing and delightful. "Wow! I could learn to appreciate this," I lustfully thought. I could not believe that I was enjoying the touch of another man. But I hadn't been touched like that by Bruce in months, and it felt good to know that my juices could still naturally flow.

My mind started playing tricks on me and without speaking a single word to Everett, I jumped up off the floor, legs queasy as ever and walked straight into the kitchen.

Once I made it into the kitchen, I braced myself on the sink for a moment and then proceeded to throw away our trash. I poured myself a nice cold drink of water and attempted to clear my mind. I stood with my back up against the counter questioning my actions.

"Oh, so this is what it feels like to be touched by another man, as a married woman," my conscience stated. "What in the hell just happened? How in the hell did that happen and just what do you think you're doing Mrs. Kyra Murrell?" My conscience asked. I couldn't understand where that kiss came from. I mean, we were just casually conversing and BAMM, just like that, I was being kissed.

At that point, I was really on edge about the rest of my weekend with Everett. Had I been a single sista, our evening would have been far different, and there's no doubt that I would have been all on him. But, I didn't know where things would go for the remainder of the evening, what to expect, or how I was going to even encourage myself to go back into that den and wrap up the evening.

This was the first time I ever had any kind of affair, so I didn't know the procedure. I had to do minutes of self-talk just to get myself back on track, not to mention what it took for me to regain my composure before facing him again. I really didn't have much of a choice about going back into the room with him. I mean, I did have a houseguest, and I couldn't just leave him sitting there for the next four days. Could I?

I decided to come up with a back-up plan, before re-entering the den. I intended to try to keep my distance for what was left of the evening, and I thought I would be safe. As long as Everett stayed on his side of the room, we might make it through the rest of the night. I gathered my courage, put my daring diva face back on and returned to the den.

"Hey you I'm back," I stated as I sat in a chair positioned slightly away from him.
"I was wondering if you had gone to bed without saying goodnight to me."

"No silly, I just had to throw away our trash and get something to drink."

"Oh! What, the drink you had in here wasn't good enough Kyra?" He sarcastically asked, while tenderly biting down on his bottom lip.

"Why are you sitting way over there," he asked. I couldn't believe that he had just asked that particular question. My first thought was to tell him, "Because I'm afraid of you." But that would have been charged against me, so instead, I replied, "I just sat here when I returned from the kitchen." He wasn't accepting that lame reply for an answer though. He had come over twelve hundred miles to see me, and there were other thoughts on his mind like affection and closeness. There was no way he was accepting my sitting so far away from him after he had waited over ninety days to hold me.

After his question, he looked at me in disbelief when I didn't move. I could tell from his mannerism that it would only be a matter of time before my back-up plan was shot out of the water. I guess he was going to allow me an opportunity to move on my own, but when I didn't, he presented the question of destruction for what I thought was a solid plan. "With all this room over here on this love seat, why don't you come over here and sit next to me, Kyra?" "HUH!!!!! My word." What was I going to say to this man at this point that would prevent me from looking wimpy? Women are far more aggressive in this day and age, than me, and here I was still acting like brotha's had to beg for some on first dates.

My conscience kicked in saying, "You can do this Kyra, just relax." I don't know how I was able to get up enough confidence to move over on that love seat next to him, but I did. "There sweetie. Now isn't that better?" He asked, while scooping my hand into his. "I've waited a long time to hold you Miss Lady and you're not going to deprive me tonight. For the past few months, all I have thought about is you and how I wanted to come here and make you feel like the woman you are. You are so beautiful, Kyra. You need to know that no matter what you are going through with Bruce; there are men out there who would have you without thinking twice and appreciate you for who you are."

I didn't respond because I didn't really know what to say. I knew my tired-ass marriage was the last topic I wanted to talk about. However, I needed to hear what he was saying and I believed his comment to be factual. I felt like tearing a little, but instead, I slumped down on the pillows and quietly sighed. He put his arms around me for comfort, pulled me closer to him and just held me, which is exactly what I needed. I think he realized how afraid of our situation I really was. He tried to reassure me that things between us would be fine and that he was only going to move as fast as I wanted him to. After listening to him, I assessed the sincerity of his comment and felt a little more relaxed. I snuggled into his arms, allowed myself to enjoy the fulfillment of being caressed and quietly thanked him. He put his finger on my lips, motioning for me to "Shhhh" and tenderly kissed my neck. How special it felt to just be held, and how refreshing it was for me to finally feel relaxed enough with him and allow myself to be in that position.

Four o'clock flashed on the DVD player, and we had both grown very tired. We were struggling to keep our eyes open, in an effort to carry the conversation much further. I suggested that we call it a night, and he was in full agreement. I escorted him to the guestroom then pulled back the comforter and sheets for him. I fluffed two big feather pillows and propped them up against the headboard of the bed, while he stripped down to his boxers. There he was slightly standing at attention, so I had to take a peek to see what he was working with. I couldn't help myself and my curiosity wouldn't have had it any other way.

"DANG!!!!!!! So, that's how Everett's doing it in the meat department," I thought. I smirked at him with this devilish look, as I handed him the remote to the television. "I'll be back soon," I stated, as I slipped away to take a shower. I went to the master bedroom on the other side of the house and pulled out some lingerie. As I tried to decide on my sleep attire, I thought about all that meat Everett was working with. I knew whatever I selected, I didn't want to be too divalicious because I didn't want to exceed the preplanned agenda for day one.

I showered, sprayed all the right spots with a dash of Arden Beauty and put on a cute, black, semi-short nighty with matching panties. I brushed my teeth, turned off the bathroom light and caught a glimpse of myself, as I passed the full-length mirror in my room. I was pleased with my selection of sleep attire, and I was sure he would be also. My nighty was sexy, but tasteful, it didn't reveal too much, and it left room for his imagination, which is exactly what I wanted.

On my way back to the guestroom, I stopped and got Everett a glass of juice. I really didn't know if he was thirsty or not, but I knew the heat was up extremely high and the house was roasting. When I walked into the room, he was knocked out. I sat the juice on the nightstand next to him and gently slid into bed. I immediately became uncomfortable with lying in bed with another man. To relax some, I pulled my top down as far as it would possibly go to make sure that any advances could be blocked. Then I pulled the covers up to my neck and this was my indirect way of telling him, "Hands Off!" However, he didn't translate the indirect message I was sending at all.

As soon as I was all snuggled in, he sprung up like a jack-in- the-box. "Hey sexy, you sure smell good," he said, while scooping me up like a rag doll and pulling me closer. He wrapped his leg over mine and held me close. Of course with all the junk in my trunk, his nature instantly became distracted and wouldn't allow him to stay focused for long. When his mind went there, I could not only feel his penis poking me in the thigh, but he broke into a mad sweat and covers went flying everywhere.

My conscience and I had become the best of friends since Everett became a part of my life. I learned to really depend on it to get me through various situations. I was in need of some encouragement and wondered where the hell it was when I needed it most. Finally, after what felt like hours, but was actually minutes, my self-talk kicked in to assist me in remaining calm.

I asked Everett if there were something I could do to make him feel a little more comfortable? He undraped his leg from across mine, and I was relieved. Well, I was until I realized where he was going next. Everett rolled over on top of me and tenderly ran his fingers through my hair. I was on the verge of screaming, when he stated, "Kyra, you have already been such an outstanding host. The only thing you could do to make me more comfortable, is relax." I thought, "RELAX! Is this Negro crazy? Here he is on top of me talking about relax." I couldn't take any more of his passion. I cupped his face in my hands, like a mother reprimanding a son and said, "You are out of control." I pushed him off of me and insisted that he get his damn hormones in check. "Everett it's really late and you need to do exactly what we came in here to do. "SLEEP!"

He made a few jokes about our present position and laughed about my nervousness. I didn't see what was so funny. In fact, I felt really silly, but I had already compromised more of my integrity than I ever imagined I would.

"Everett, those Busy Hands of yours move way too fast for me," I cynically stated. I could tell that he felt a little guilty about his actions after my comment, so he apologized for his behavior, tenderly pecked my lips and fell asleep. I laid in bed restless for hours, but once I talked myself down and stopped staring into the darkness, I was able to relax and fell asleep as well.

Early that Friday morning before he woke up, I slipped out of bed and propped his second card up against a glass sitting on the kitchen counter. When he came into the kitchen that morning, I wanted my card to be the first thing he saw. I tried not to disturb him, but when I walked into the bedroom to get my robe, I noticed that he was lying in bed with his eyes open.

"Hey Busy Hands, did you sleep well?" I asked.
He smiled at the nickname and replied,
"I could have slept a little better if you had held me like I wanted
you to." I wasn't touching that comment because it could have gone
anywhere.

Everett got out of the bed and started over my way. He reached
out, grabbed me and hugged me from behind. I quickly noticed his
slight erection and commented on the warmth of his body.
"I did hold you through the night, but I backed away from you
because your body was hot and you were sweating like crazy."
"Is that why you're up so early Ky, because I had you hot,"
I gave him this look and went on with what I was doing. I could see
that our conversation was once again about to go somewhere I
wasn't ready to venture.

It was hopeless, his mind was gutter bound. He must have been
an early morning nookie man because everything I said sent him
there. No matter what I said, he couldn't get sex off his mind.
Everything stimulated a sexual response, and he had too many signs
of a brotha in need of some early morning romance. Plus, I was still
walking around in my pajamas, and he couldn't get his mind or his
eyes off my ass. I think he was on the verge of trying to get him
some and that was way off the agenda, so I knew we had to hurry
up and get out of the house.

"Come on, let's get dressed so we can get on this highway before
it gets too late," I said, while clapping my hands. He extended his
arms to hug me, but I pushed them down and told him a clean towel
was waiting in the bathroom for him. Just as Everett turned to walk
to the bathroom, the phone rang and startled me. I looked at the ID
box and it was Bruce.

"It's Bruce." I whispered, as I reached for the phone and
answered.
"Hello!"
"Hey Kyra."

"Hey Bruce."

"Where have you been? I called a few times yesterday and earlier this morning and got no answer."

"Well, I was out late last night at my sorority meeting. Afterwards, a few of my sorors and I stood around talking in the parking lot. When you called this morning, I was in the shower. I tried to get the phone, but you had already hung up."

"Oh, well I'm working in the field this morning. I took a short break to check in with you and say hello. Kiss the baby for me and I'll call you two later."

"Ok, bye," I replied as I hung up the phone and went on with my business like I didn't have a conscience at all.

It kind of frightened me to think that I could be so dogmatic. I guess that is just where we were in our relationship. I know one thing for sure, I didn't feel bad about the pleasure another man was bringing into my life, and I couldn't understand where that attitude was coming from. It scared me to know that I had become that kind of bitch, but it wasn't like I never tried to prevent myself from going there. I asked myself, "What kind of woman am I becoming and am I ready to be this woman?" I wasn't sure about my response either way and that terrified me the most.

7

Dallas, Texas

Once we got on the highway, we had about a three-hour drive ahead of us. We found all types of stimulating subjects to keep us busy while we traveled. As we drove through Gainesville, Texas, we stopped at the Gainesville Outlet Mall to look around. Now that I was out of Oklahoma, I found myself much more relaxed with Everett. The fear I initially had of running into someone I knew wasn't quite as intense and our time together flowed much better.

My experience at the mall with Everett is one I will never forget. Once we parked, I got out of the car, hit the remote keypad to lock the doors and met him at the front of the car. There he was with his arm extended, waiting for me to grab his hand. When our hands touched, it felt like magic and my hands began to tingle. It made me think of the affection my husband once displayed towards me when we were in love. At this point in our marriage, Bruce wouldn't dare walk around the mall holding my hand because he had become too stiff and uptight for that.

Initially, I felt uneasy about walking around, holding hands with Everett. But, as I walked from store-to-store, I relaxed a little more and our date became easier to enjoy. We entered the food court and walked up on a lottery ticket booth. I loved scratching lottery tickets, so I eagerly suggested that we buy a few and try our luck. We bought six dollars worth of tickets; then, I sat down on a brick wall right in front of the booth to wait for him to find some change. He pulled two coins out of his pocket, giving one to me and keeping the other for himself. "Kyra, before we scratch these tickets we need to agree that whoever wins will split their winnings fifty-fifty." I laughed at his suggestion, because it was nice to think that had he won one dollar, he was willing to give me fifty cent of his earnings.

Neither of us won anything and the loser lottery ticket adventure grew old quick. "Well that's that Everett, better luck next time," I stated while pitching my tickets into the trash. He threw his tickets away as well, bought something to drink, and then we walked back to the car.

Once we were back on the road, he draped his arm over the armrest, cupped my hand in his, reclined his seat and settled in for the ride into Dallas. He kissed my right hand a few times and frequently rubbed his tongue across my fingers. As I attempted to stay focused on the road, he began to kiss and gently suck my index finger, which turned me on. As he moved from one finger to the next, my stomach became queasy. I started visualizing him sucking my fingers in the same manner, while making passionate love to me. "Oh hell naw Kyra. You're not making love to this man on his first visit," my conscience quickly chimed in.

This charismatic man was simply too much for me and had completely won me over. He had me feeling great, and he knew it. It was obvious to us both that he had me very distracted. I had become sexually aroused and needed to pull over for a restroom run. But, he was a little arrogant about his abilities to please me, and I didn't want to confirm what he thought he already knew. Yeah he had me hot, but after he made a few remarks, I was cautious about not getting caught up on feeding his ego.

We made it to the Galleria early enough to enjoy a little shopping and watch some children ice skating in the rink, centrally located in the mall. There was a luxurious Westin Hotel linked to the mall also, so we decided to stay there. As we walked to the hotel entrance, we passed a number of upscale franchises. While passing Tiffany's, I commented on their perfume being my most favorite fragrance and before I could finish my sentence, Everett had turned us around and we were in the store making a purchase.

Once in the hotel the staff working the front desk thought we were married and commented on what a lovely couple we made. We both just kind of laughed to ourselves, while walking to the elevator. "If they only knew," I mumbled to him under my breath, while stepping into the elevator.

We rode the elevator alone from the lobby up to the twenty-third floor. Once the double doors shut, I pushed the button for our floor and Everett was all over me. He eased up on me until my back was up against the elevator wall. He slightly spread his legs, to make himself level with me, licked my nose and kissed my lips. While we were hugging, I noticed a reflection of the back of his head on the elevator door. Shortly after, I noticed that I was caressing his head with my right hand and stroking his neck with the left. I wanted to savor that moment, but a sparkling reflection on the elevator door interrupted my fantasy.

The three-karat diamond on my wedding band was killing the moment. The part of my conscience that still had a little hope for my marriage kicked in. It tried to distract my moment of ecstasy, but I wasn't having it. "Oh shut up," I thought and my conscience quickly understood. If the glistening reflection of my wedding ring was supposed to detour me and serve as a reminder of my commitment to Bruce, it didn't. I pulled Mr. Barnett closer to me, closed my eyes, relaxed my lips, and gave him the kiss that he so deservingly earned.

That particular kiss could have lasted forever, but the elevator reached the twenty-third floor and the doors slowly opened. "This is our floor," I stated, as I grabbed my bag and headed for the room. Once we made it to the door, Everett slid the electronic key into the slot, and I turned the handle. "After you, Kyra." Everett whispered, as he held the door open for me to enter first. The large living area and super king size bed in the bedroom was awesome. I had never seen a bed quite that large in my life. However, for what we were paying to stay there, something worth remembering was a mandatory requirement.

Falling on the bed face first was my first thought. But, remembering a news report I saw earlier in the year prevented that from happening. There was no way I was laying my face on a comforter that might have contained thirteen different sperm samples. Instead, I walked up to Everett, put my arms around his neck, thanked him for coming to see me and gently pecked his lips. "Are you ready to get something to eat?" He asked. I nodded my head, "yes" and we headed back out of the room to the elevators.

Once again, we rode down to the lobby alone, and once again, he was all over me initiating kisses. I remember him backing away from me to ask with this adorable expression on his face,
"Why you kissing me?"
"Kissing you, you're kissing me," I replied.

In the restaurant that evening, we had cocktails and ate a real light spinach dip with tortilla chips. The majority of the time, we spent reminiscing, and talking about plans for future visits. Three hours had come and gone like a peaceful rain. It didn't seem as though we had been in Bennigan's talking that long. But because we found ourselves in such good company once again, we completely lost track of time. I knew Everett was ready for some one-on-one adventures, but I had other things in mind once we made it back to the room.

Once we were back in the room, I pulled out a deck of cards, which I thought he would enjoy. I wanted to expose him to my competitive side. I explained my version of the rules for Tunk and could see that he had given me his undivided attention. While listening, he closely observed the motion of my lips, as if he were studying them. At times, he almost appeared to be consumed in my every word. I wondered if he was really listening or just pretending to be. "Did you get all of those instructions," I asked. And with the most passionate look in his eyes and this lustful expression on his face, he replied, "Sure did sexy."

We played one round and he was no longer interested in playing games. He sat back in his chair, tapped on his knees and motioned with his head for me to come and sit on his lap. I knew I needed to proceed with caution because this man had quick hands, and as emotionally starved as I had been, I knew I wasn't any match for him, nor was I up for the challenge.

As weak as I felt, I didn't know what else I could do to prevent myself from getting sexed down that evening. Within the past two days, I had already had far more than the reasonable amount of self-talks a woman could endure to keep herself out of trouble, and I was tired of debating with myself. I needed some affection and I wanted to be close to him, so I slowly got up and moved over to his chair. I draped my legs over his thighs and sat down in his lap.

There was some real passion in the room when he looked into my eyes with those beautiful hazel eyes of his. He moistened his lips and I immediately knew exactly what was about to go down. He moved his head forward to kiss me, and I could only kiss him back. There was nothing that I could think of to prevent me from wanting to kiss him. Not even the thought of being married with a husband who financially provided extremely well for his family.

While he held me in his arms, my heart throbbed. Everett made me feel like a princess in every manner of the word. He didn't realize what he was doing in my life at that time, but he was mending my lonely, broken heart and teaching me how to relax and appreciate being desired by a man again.

I couldn't restrain myself much longer, and I realized that I needed to do something to change the mood. I expressed that I was getting tired and slowly got up off of his lap to give him time to get his "jewels" in order. I walked straight into the bathroom and prepared the water for my shower. I pulled out my bath gel and perfume, a t-shirt, and some accessories. I checked the water temperature one additional time then stripped down to my underclothes. I realized right as I was about to get into the shower that I had left my cosmetic bag on the bed.

When I walked into the bedroom in my panties and bra to get my bag, I laughed to myself, as I noticed Everett's expression once he focused on my butt. He bit his lips and had the naughtiest smirk on his face. After his look, I couldn't resist teasing him, so back and forth I went from the room to the bathroom getting this and looking for that. I had given him such an eye full that he had a full fledge erection by the time I finished. Finally I stopped in mid-stride, looked over at him and said,

"Care to join me?"

"Hell yeah," he replied and quickly sprung up off the bed like someone who had sat on hot coals. He hadn't moved quite that fast all weekend. When I finally made it into the bathroom myself, he was already butt naked and had beaten me into the shower.

The water beat against my back, while we held each other in the shower. Everett stood behind me in the tub to make sure that most of the water hit me first, and I know he was freezing because my arms were.

"Baby, I'm crazy about you." He stated.

"Well Everett, I'd like to think that you didn't just make this trip just because you wanted to freeze your butt off in the back of a shower."

"You're so silly, and I hope you know that you just killed the moment." I laughed, while slapping him on his butt and replying.

"Come on, get up here in this water before you catch a nasty cold."

Everett rinsed the soap off of his body and got out of the shower. As for me, my conscience was back in full effect and cock blocking like crazy. I stayed in the shower for an additional thirty minutes, hoping he would be asleep when I finally came out. But, that was foolish thinking on my behalf because when I walked out of the bathroom, Everett and his "manhood" were wide-awake. He was patiently lying there waiting on me and was up in every manner.

"Hey babe! I see you waited up for me," I sarcastically stated.
"Yeah ,we sure did," he replied.

We both had to laugh because he knew where I was coming from with my comment. As I walked over to my side of the bed, I noticed a little hand towel on the nightstand. My brain instantly went into think mode. "I know this sucka don't think he's about to get some ass on the first visit."

I crawled into bed, and pulled the covers over my body. I didn't want to have the same kind of experience as the night before.
"You're going to be fine tonight. You didn't send any mixed messages in the shower and you two have been on the same page all day." I told myself before relaxing.

Seconds after my self-talk shut down and tucked me in for the night .....Busy Hands came to life. Everett scooped me up just like he had the night before. However, I wasn't as nervous as the first night because I knew what to expect. I also knew that he wouldn't go too far if I asked him to stop. But, I was still extremely uncomfortable.

What made me most nervous was when he moved up on me, and raw reproductive meat stabbed me all in my stomach and thighs. I damn near jumped out of the bed, but considered that the only thing I really needed to do was move in the opposite direction, and brace myself.

I thought, "This man is in the bed butt naked and has clearly lost his mind." Once I endured all I could, for as long as I could, which was all of five minutes. I cupped his face once again and repeated the famous five words from the night before. "You are out of control."

8

Wine and Feet

The next morning, I woke up early to put out his third card entitled "Very." I opened the curtains to let some sun in, flopped on the bed and laid my head against his chest. There I was looking into his resting face, admiring his every feature. From the curve of his lips to his well-groomed facial hair, this man really had it goin on. I pondered on the relationship we had involved ourselves in, wondering where we would go from that point, if anywhere.

I immediately found myself day dreaming about future encounters with Everett. I wondered, "Could I fall in love with him and should he fall in love with me?" Most of all I wondered if I could offer him any kind of a real relationship. I knew I shouldn't worry myself too much with that issue because one thing that came out in our conversation over dinner was the fact that he was involved. His girlfriend, Kimberlin, lived in Chicago and was in the process of trying to relocate to Detroit. He didn't provide a definite date, or the fact that it was a definite decision on her behalf. However, I listened to him when he talked about her, and due to his loneliness, I could tell that he was anxious for her to move, though he never said it.

I didn't know what to think about the situation but, I knew if she had good sense, she better move closer to her fine ass man. If she didn't, at the rate we were going, he was going to be in love with me. I was going to make sure of that. In my heart, I knew she would move sooner or later, but it was my hopes that it would be later. I needed some time to enjoy him all to myself without distractions, which she would have been, once she moved to Detroit.

Realistically, I knew the best decision I could make was for me to back away and try to establish a great friendship with him. But I really wanted more because a friendship didn't seem like enough for me. Actually, after interacting with him for the past few months on a regular basis, I seriously wanted to be with him.

"Stop thinking so much and just enjoy the weekend," I kept telling myself. But, I felt like an addict, hooked on the attention he provided. Though my needs were being taken care of for the moment, my main concern was the next opportunity I would have to see him again.

While I continued to adore him, he started to cough and my thoughts were interrupted. "Are you ok babe? Would you like for me to get you a glass of water?" I asked. He raised his head with squinted eyes and replied, "Yes, please." I poured him a glass of water, and he gently caressed my hand, as I handed him his drink. He tilted the glass up to his mouth and drank until it was completely empty. "UMMMMMMMMMMMMM, just fine," is all I could think, as I sat there watching him lick a drop of water from his bottom lip.

He couldn't go back to sleep after he finished his drink, so we just held each other for a while and talked about our mates. He was a little hesitant to talk about Kimberlin at first, but I assured him that it was okay with me for him to openly discuss her. He cautiously shared facts regarding their relationship, while I too was very reserved to talk about my relationship with Bruce. We covered some real touchy subjects, but I was most displeased with the outcome of our discussion about us. Neither of us had the answer for our situation. However, we were both certain that we wanted to continue to be a part of each other's lives.

After hours of talking, Everett and I were both finally talked out. The early afternoon had quickly arrived, so we decided to get up, get dressed and take advantage of the rest of the day. Everett was still naked from the night before, and I was curious as to how he was going to get out of bed in order to get dressed. There was absolutely no shame in his game. He removed the covers, and crawled out of bed like he was wearing PJ's with his manhood flopping everywhere.

Taking Everett on a tour of Dallas was my primary reason for bringing him to Texas. Once we got out of the hotel, our first stop took us to the beautiful skyscrapers of downtown Dallas. There was some kind of festival going on that weekend, so we parked far out and walked back to the main attraction. Hand-in-hand we walked, like a real couple, stopping in different gift shops and snacking along the way. We took a few pictures here and there for the sake of capturing the moment, but neither of us knew what we would do with them afterwards. I surely couldn't take mine home, and he was basically in the same position. He joked about locking them up in a safe he had at his house, but I never took him seriously. We didn't want anything to spoil the adventure we were having, so we really didn't worry too much about what to do with the photos. Savoring the occasion was most important, so we did just that.

We continued to admire the skyscrapers, birds, billowy clouds and the rich blue tone in the sky that afternoon. There were so many different attractions to admire on Main Street and so little time to see everything. Hours of walking around in the cold had taken a toll on me. My feet were hurting and my skin itched from all the walking in the cold weather. We agreed to finish up our tour a little early and walked back to the car.

"So, what do you want to do from here," I asked.

"Actually, I've seen enough of Texas. We could head back to Oklahoma City today and find something there to get into. That way, we wouldn't have to travel so early Sunday morning to get me to the airport."

I had forgotten all about him flying out that Sunday. I totally agreed with the suggestion to avoid an early morning drive back. It was far more convenient to get him to Will Rogers World Airport from Oklahoma City, so we checked out of our hotel, made our way to I-35 north and arrived in Oklahoma City at seven o'clock that evening. Before going to the house, we stopped by the liquor store and agreed on a bottle of red wine. Selecting a brand caused a slight problem. He liked his wine dry and I liked mine sweet. I would have compromised, but I knew under no circumstances would I drink dry wine; I hated it with a passion. The store salesman attempted to be the mediator for us and suggested a few brands. Finally, after minutes of debating we agreed on a bottle of Zinfandels.

While driving home, I thought of some different kinds of activities I could do to entertain him. My entire agenda was originally planned for Texas, but I was flexible. Once we made it to the house, I put my luggage in the room, while Everett poured two glasses of wine. I slipped into the den, lit two candles and proceeded to make the environment a romantic one. I turned on some Brian McKnight, filled a foot spa with water and called Everett into the room. I remember how he walked around the corner smiling with a glass of wine in each hand. I patted the chair cushion and insisted that he sit down. I then rested his legs on my knees, and removed his shoes and socks.

Wouldn't you know it; this man had the most gorgeous feet, too. They were flawless, except for a few pieces of lint, which I picked off and then placed his feet into the foot spa. I gave Everett a sixty-minute pedicure and foot message he will never forget as long as he is African-American. He sat back with his head resting against the back of the chair and slowly sipped his wine with his eyes closed. All that was missing from the scene was a crown because I know I made him feel like a king.

While rubbing foot cream on the heels of his feet, I stated, "Wine and feet on a Saturday evening. What a combination." When there was no reply I looked up at Everett, and he was knocked out. The pedicure must have been just what the doctor ordered or Everett was extremely exhausted. When I tried to wake him, he couldn't keep his eyes open for anything. I left him resting in the den, while I watched the last of a basketball game in my bedroom. At about one in the morning, I finally woke him up and encouraged him to get in bed. I was tired as well, so I put his fourth and final card entitled "Much" on his luggage and went to bed in my room.

That next morning, as I relaxed in bed, I reflected over the weekend. I was glad that we had the opportunity to spend some quality time together, but I was also somewhat discouraged that it was Sunday and our time together was coming to an end. I was quite satisfied with Everett's visit. But, after spending a weekend that special with another man, I couldn't help but think about Bruce also. He hadn't called since that Friday morning. The saddest part about that was that I didn't seem to miss him one bit, nor did I realize that he had not checked in until that moment.

He must have been somewhere lying up with one of his other women. I suppose he was too busy romancing her to worry about what was going on with me. When he was away from home on weekend business, his calls were usually limited anyway. I had grown used to not hearing from him, so the fact that he hadn't called, didn't seem to bother me much. However, the thought of him not calling, due to the possibility of being occupied in the same manner in which I had been, pissed me off. The more I thought about not talking to Bruce over the weekend, the more I convinced myself that it was probably best. If we had spoken, he would have only said something to irritate me. His mission would have been accomplished and that would have just demolished a perfectly great weekend for Everett, and me.

Everything about Sunday went by so quickly. Before our day really even started, we were sitting around in the airport reminiscing over the past few days. He changed the subject and left me speechless when he said he wanted to see me again in a few weeks. "Ah Ha," I thought. "So this man is capable of falling for me." I smiled as I wondered what kind of sick twisted pleasure I had gotten out of that confirmation. I didn't seriously think that I could have a long-term romance with him under the circumstances. But, I thought it would be adventurous to see how interested in me he really was. I called myself calling his bluff, but in the end, he called mine.

"Sure, whenever you want to do this again, call me." I replied.

"No need to call you, I'll be back in two weeks."

"Right, you'll be back in two weeks, and I'll hold my breath."

"I can show you better than I can tell you. Hold your breath if you like. What you'll discover is that I'm serious about you."

"Well Mr. Barnett, I guess you'll just have to show me, then. I don't believe for a minute that you're coming back in two weeks"

"Ok, well I'm going to show you." He replied.

Everett got up from his seat, walked to the ticket counter and purchased his ticket for the second visit. I was impressed as I shook my head at him once he returned to his seat and placed the tickets in my hand.

"Don't test me, Kyra, cause I ain't no joke. I do what I say and say what I mean," he replied with this "Now What" smirk on his face. I smiled big from ear to ear because I knew I had just been called out.

He looked at his watch and noticed the time. He kissed my hand, and then hugged me real tight. "I had such a good time with you Kyra, and I can't wait to see you in two weeks." I felt the sincerity in his words and I didn't want to let him go. I knew he had to catch his plane, so I hugged him one last time and slowly backed away. I could tell he wanted to kiss me. I wanted to kiss him too, but I wasn't stupid or that bold, so I affectionately rubbed his hands and waved goodbye.

He maintained eye contact for a second. Suddenly, without looking back, he turned and headed down the terminal. I watched him briefly, but my heart started to feel lonely again. He had been such great company for me for the past few days. I cringed at the thought of having to go back to the reality of my life with Bruce and the bullshit I was going through with him. As I turned and walked to the car, my head hung in sorrow. I could immediately feel the void for companionship overwhelming me.

I walked as far as the parking lot, when I decided I had to call Everett's cell phone. By the time I called, he had already turned it off. My phone beeped, but it was just my voicemail alerting me of a message stored on my phone. When I checked my messages, Everett had already left a message for me. He was thinking as I and had left me a mushy "Miss You" message. "Hey baby, this is Busy Hands. I just wanted you to know that I'm missing you like crazy already. I'll see you in two weeks, and I'll call you when my plane lands."

9

What Am I Gonna Do

Everett and I were talking quite frequently after he returned to Detroit. Since he had already purchased his second plane ticket, we found ourselves anxious and counting down the days again. As the days slowly ticked by, I tried to think of some unique ideas I could do for his visit. All that week, I pondered over ideas I could do to make our second encounter just as special as the first. I wanted his every encounter with me to be like a fairytale. Huh! But, isn't that the primary purpose for getting involved in an affair to begin with?

Bruce was leaving that Friday morning for his annual corporate meeting in Houston, Texas and would be gone until the following Tuesday. Taylor was going to his sister's house for the weekend because they had family coming in from out-of- town. I spent Thursday evening packing a weekend bag for her and sporadically arguing with Bruce about who he was seeing on the side. He denied being involved in an affair, but I didn't believe him. I had scheduled an appointment with Perkins Enterprise, which was a PI firm in Oklahoma City for that Friday morning. I planned to hire someone to trail Bruce and provide me with some concrete evidence for a divorce. I was uncertain about my feelings for him, but as long as we were married, I wasn't in favor of him tipping out with another woman.

Friday morning started with a beautiful sunrise. It also marked the day of Everett's arrival. I eagerly drove to my appointment at Perkins Enterprise and then to work. That entire day at work, I watched the clock. Everett's plane was due in at nine forty that evening. I was barely doing any work and decided to leave a little early to prepare for his visit. I still had a few last minute errands to run, and I wanted to make sure that my special evening with him went off without error. I grabbed my purse out of my desk drawer and rushed to the detailing shop to have my car cleaned. I probably could have passed on a car wash because my car wasn't really that dirty. But, I really didn't want to have a man as sexy as him cruising the city in a dirty car.

While waiting in the lobby of Dwayne's Detailing Shop for my car to be cleaned, I ran into my ex-boy friend, Calvin. Calvin Fulton was still a very handsome, deep dark chocolate brotha. He was the type of brotha who knew he was fine and spent more time in the mirror than I did, which was one of his biggest flaws when we were an item. I watched him out of the corner of my eye, as he approached me.

"What is this punk about to come over here and say to me," I wondered.

"Hey beautiful! You sure are looking really gorgeous in your older age."

"Well thank you Calvin," I replied as snooty as I possibly could. I still hadn't forgiven him from our past breakup. I was quite bitter and not in the mood to be bothered.

"What have you been doing?" He asked with the warmest smile on his face. I smirked, as I thought to myself before replying to his question, "I know this Negro doesn't think that we're friends, or even remotely cool like that, for that matter." But to maintain my classiness, I cordially replied,

"I haven't been up to too much of anything, Calvin. I have just been working, being a wife and a Mom."

"Yeah! Congratulations Kyra, I heard that you had gotten yourself married. Are you happy?"

I looked at him with the most ignorant expression on my face. I wanted to tell him to, "Move the hell around!" But instead I took advantage of the opportunity to rub his nose in his loss. "Yeah, I'm very happy. Marriage requires work just like any other relationship, but you wouldn't know anything about working it out. Those words didn't seem to exist in your vocabulary. You only knew words like tricks, hanging out with the fellas and creepin, remember!"

He looked so shaken from my response. I must have really stunned him with my comment because he was all prepared to talk me to death until that point. He became visibly irritated with our conversation. At that point, he abruptly replied, "It was good seeing you again, Kyra. Here's my number, please call me sometime." I wondered why he would want me to call him considering our break up and the manner in which I had spoken to him. I considered telling him while he was all up in my face sweating me, that my damn name wasn't "Tweet" and I wouldn't be calling." But, I simply replied, "No thanks, I'll pass," then I gave him the cold shoulder.

After my reply, I noticed him slipping his number into the side pocket of my purse. I was about to go there, when a young man working in the shop informed me that my car was ready. I abruptly got up from my seat. "Have a great day, Calvin," I said, as I opened the waiting room door to exit.

"You do the same beautiful. Work on that bitterness too. You are much too adorable to still be holding a grudge."

"Oh, don't worry; I'm going to work on it today," I replied. As I walked out of the door, I looked back at him to make sure that he was watching me and once we made eye contact; I took his number out of my purse and threw it in the trash.

Calvin didn't appreciate me when I was his woman, and I'm sure he hadn't changed much since we separated, so why in the world would I waste my time and energy back tracking? I almost got mad at the thought of him trying to play me. But, thoughts of Everett invaded my mind, which caused me to relax while driving to the mall. Once I arrived, I went into the department store to pick up a pair of Tommy boxers. I also purchased a bottle of Phat Farm Cologne and two cards. As a joke, I purchased a pair of seductive panties; then, I left the mall in a rush to get to the liquor store to buy a bottle of Cognac.

I made it to the house with Everett's things at about seven that evening. I decided to put all the nick-knacks I purchased in a gift basket for his second visit. Of course my creativity kicked in once again. This visit was going to be just as wonderful as the first had been. He was going to love that Gift Basket more than he enjoyed getting a card each day because I had named it the "BUSY HANDS" starter kit.

I completed two beautiful cards and in one of them, I enclosed the pair of panties. I sprayed them with a hint of Miracle perfume to make sure he remembered the fragrance I wore the weekend of our second visit. Not to mention that I also wanted him to have something in Detroit that reminded him of me.

Because I wanted to add some adventure to our visit, I decided that I would give him the card with the panties in the airport. The second card, which remained in the car with the rest of his gifts read, "Nothing turns me on more than a sexy man, with bedroom eyes and a gorgeous smile. Well! Except for a sexy man with those two features, in some Tommy boxers, smelling good, and sipping on some Remy."

His plane arrived a little late, but like our last visit I was still just as thrilled to see him. I watched him as he walked up the terminal with that walk of his. Once he approached me, we briefly hugged and headed to baggage claim. I handed him the card, which included the seductive panties as we made it to the down escalator. He opened the card while he was walking to the carrousel to get his luggage, and the panties fell out. With excitement in his voice, he asked,

"DAMN!!!!!!!! What are these, Kyra? Do you plan on modeling them for me tonight?"

"No, but I might let you eat them off of me," I friskily replied.

"That sounds real good to me. Is that a promise or are you just talking shit?"

"You already know the answer freak, so don't even go there." I replied.

Those panties stayed on his mind, the entire time we stood around waiting on his luggage. He kept asking me how they would tie into the evening. I never gave him an answer. I just kept this devious smile on my face, while occasionally winking at him. After retrieving only one of his bags off the conveyer belt, he soon discovered that some of his luggage had been lost. We walked over to the airline claim office and reported his lost bag to the attendant.

"We apologize for the inconvenience Mr. Barnett. Someone will be contacting you, once your luggage arrives with a delivery time," the attendant stated.

Everett clutched the one bag that arrived in his hand, while we walked to the car. I was beaming as we walked through the parking garage. Everett didn't realize how much I missed him, but I hoped that I could show him how special he had become to me.

"Hey you! Do you know that I have been missing you so much," I stated, as I leaned forward and tenderly kissed him on his cheek.

"Yeah! Me too," he replied with an expression on his face that only we could appreciate. "Kyra, I guess we can just go straight to the hotel, get checked in and go from there. I need to shower and get out of this monkey suit, so I can feel a little more comfortable."

I initially wanted to take him out for a night on the town, since it didn't happen during his first visit. But my plans for the night weren't going to happen due to his lost luggage. We went by the family store to pick up some personal items then headed to the hotel. We checked into our suite about twelve o'clock in the morning. Everett slumped down on the bed looking totally disgusted.

"I can't believe they lost my damn bag."

"I'm sorry baby, maybe it will get in early."

"Yeah I hope so, if it doesn't we're going shopping because I'm not waiting around all day." He stated while walking into the bathroom.

He showered, sprayed on a little Premier cologne, put on his boxers, a sweater and the only pair of slacks that arrived with him that evening. He poured himself a glass of cognac and sat on the ottoman between my legs, facing me. That brotha smelled good and was looking F...I...N...E. He showered me with so much affection that I actually pulled hairs on my arm to make sure that I was not dreaming. The time I spent with him was like an untold fairytale waiting to unravel. The question I had to ask myself was, "If I was ready for the climax of our story?" My reply, "I wasn't exactly sure," but I was ready to at least reap some of the benefits that came along with being one of the main characters.

He rubbed my outer thighs, and I immediately got goose bumps and chills all over my body. He licked my lips like a Popsicle, while looking into my face. I couldn't help staring at his mouth. Those beautiful lips of his were calling out my name. It was hard to stay focused on his conversation because I intently looked at his lips in lust the entire time we conversed. The physical attraction I had for him was causing me to feel as though I had certainly gotten in over my head. I couldn't redirect my feelings for him, and I wondered quite frequently, "What I was going to do?" This man just tiptoed into my life, caused me to feel like a woman again and made me believe that I needed him. What I was currently feeling for him felt damn good to my soul and even though I knew it was wrong to feel the way I did about him, I desperately needed what he contributed to my life.

Bruce had been starving me of the attention and affection I truly needed and deserved. It felt good to be complimented, caressed and appreciated. I convinced myself that I wasn't willing to give up the only male companion who finally brought some kind of satisfaction into my world. So, since Everett was giving me what I needed, it was up to me to keep things in their proper prospective. I was married and no matter how much I wanted to be with Everett, I couldn't give him one hundred percent of what he deserved or desired from a woman. I had no choice but to stay focused.

There were times when I slipped into a superficial, dream world and it was getting the best of me emotionally. After evaluating our situation, I told myself that night, that I would enjoy the remainder of our weekend and after he left on Sunday, I would totally terminate our relationship.

Early that Saturday morning my cell phone rang. It was Bruce, and I was actually surprised to hear from him that early on a weekend. He informed me that he was going to be home from Houston that Sunday night, instead of Tuesday. He needed a ride from the airport, and he wanted me to pick him up about seven o'clock.

"That's fine. I'll see you then Bruce."
"You seem to be in a rush Kyra."
"No actually, when you called, you woke me up out of a deep sleep."
"Well I guess I better let you get back to sleep then."

After discontinuing our conversation, I propped my pillow against Everett's arm and tried to go back to sleep. My thoughts were distracted after speaking with Bruce as usual. He seemed to have a way of calling at the most awkward times and completely changing my mood. I laid there in Everett's arms for the longest time, thinking, "How in the world could you love someone so much one day and wake up the next day complete strangers." I had no real answers or solutions for the situation between Bruce and I. I only knew that our situation was really damaged, and we were desperately in need of professional help.

I had become totally restless and kept shifting my body from one side to the other. I was in search of a comfortable position, but wasn't having any luck finding one. I must have disturbed Everett with all of the shifting because he finally asked me, after minutes of tossing and turning if I were okay. I wiped my eyes and expressed my degree of unhappiness with Bruce. The more I talked about my troubled marriage, the more my eyes filled with fresh tears. Finally, with one blink, tears fell from my eyes like a semi-heavy rain.

He attentively listened to my sorrows, provided his input and never degraded Bruce once as a husband. He never projected his opinion on my marriage, nor did he make any suggestions about what he thought I should do. He just kept telling me, "Talk with your husband when he returns home and you will know what's best for you and your family. The answers may not come instantly Kyra, but give yourself time to process everything that has been happening in your life. When it's time, you'll make the right decision for Taylor and yourself. Nobody can tell you what's best for you. You have to come to that conclusion on your own." I realized what Everett was saying was right. I tried to dry my eyes, though tears continued to occasionally fall. He hugged me and stroked my hair, as I laid in his arms for comfort and once I regained my composure I fell asleep watching television.

We were supposed to get out early, but we waited on the airline to deliver Everett's luggage. By the time they finally arrived, we had both taken a shower, and I was almost dressed. We finally got out about one-thirty that afternoon. I was anxious to show Everett my place of employment and give him a tour of the department I supervised for International Affairs. Once we left the hotel, we drove to my office before doing anything else. I knew no one would be working in my department on a Saturday, so I wasn't nervous about taking him into the building. Once we arrived, cleared security and made it to the seventh floor, much to my surprise, I discovered that a few of my employees had come in to catch up on some past due work.

Gail, one of my casual friends who had recently experienced a divorce of her own, and the Assistant Director of my department was really checking Everett out. "Hey Girl! And might I ask just who is this handsome fellow you're with?" I turned a little pale after she presented her question to me. First of all, I was a little shocked that she even had the nerve to ask me such a question, and secondly, I wanted to tell her, none of her damn business. But, instead of being rude, I introduced Everett as my cousin.

The word cousin was like the lonely, female password. From that reply alone, the other two women in the office started dropping bids on him as well. They started inquiring about how they could get a little one-on-one time with him, and they wanted me to set them up. I leaned over and jokingly whispered to Everett, "These woman are desperate. Don't be fooled. It has nothing to do with your sex appeal. And you have one time to try and talk to any one of these tricks and I'm giving you a fat lip."

A few times they almost caused me to get down right indignant, but I knew I had to keep my composure. Gail was all up in Everett's face. She never considered the fact that he might be my chippie. But, I knew that wasn't a thought that crossed her mind. She was always teasing me about Bruce and I being the "Perfect Couple."

I couldn't watch these women carry on like they were any longer. I finally decided enough was enough and backed them up off of Everett by replying,
"Sorry ladies, get your hormones in check. My sexy cuz is in a committed relationship. I happen to love his woman and she doesn't need any Oklahoma drama in her life."
"Ohhhhhhhh! Kyra's hatin," Gail jokingly stated.
"Well you and the rest of the office hoochies are acting like you're desperate."

They all looked at Everett as if they were waiting for him to agree or disagree, but he knew it was best to keep quiet and that's exactly what he did.

10

Cat Got Your Tongue

The chemistry between Everett and I was perfect. It seemed to keep us both feeling like we needed to have more and more of each other's time. It also allowed me to let my guard down a bit, be myself and do whatever came natural. That Saturday evening we went out to dinner. I wasn't much of a drinker, but sometimes I socially drank with friends. I ordered two Mudslides and each of them seemed to be prepared with far more liquor than I preferred. By the time I ate my meal and sucked down my two drinks, I was feeling just right. My buzz was nice, my head was light, my eyes were playing tricks on me and I felt like doing something fun.

"Let's go play darts," I suggested.

"Darts," he repeated.

"Yeah, you know the little oblong things you throw at a score board."

"I'm ready for a different kind of game, Kyra. Maybe we could go back to the hotel and play a game that I've mastered."

"Well what if I've mastered that game too?"

"Then we're going to have some real competition going on in our suite tonight." He replied, as he pulled me towards the door to exit the restaurant.

As we drove back to the room, I was still feeling the effects of my buzz. I pulled over and had him drive the remainder of the way. Once he sat in the driver's seat, he grabbed my left hand, caressed my fingers and drove us back to the hotel. "Kyra, I have really enjoyed spending time with you and no matter what happens between us, please promise me that we will always be friends." I assured him that if we found ourselves in too deep and had to retreat from the relationship to save our friendship, so be it, we would do just that. I also mentioned that I was contemplating terminating our special friendship, which sent him into deep thought. I was slightly tempted to ask, what was on his mind, but instead, I remained silent and allowed him to process his thoughts without any disturbances. I could have asked a zillion questions, but sometimes questions shouldn't be asked. And though, I desired to know his thoughts, I didn't have the nerve to ask anyway because I feared his reply.

He pulled into the hotel parking lot, took up two parking spaces, and shut off the headlights. He sat at the steering wheel silent for a moment and then stated, "If you weren't married, you know you'd be my woman on a full time basis, don't you?" I heard him, but I didn't really hear him. His comment took a moment to register and before I could even respond or acknowledge his statement, he opened his door and got out. I sat there for a brief second trying to make sure I heard him correctly.

Finally, I reached for the door handle, but before I could pull it, he was already opening the door to let me out. "What are you still sitting there for, Kyra? Has the cat got your tongue or did I catch you off guard with my comment," he asked, as he reached for my hand to help me out of the car.

We walked to the back entrance of the hotel and as usual, I was at a loss for words. For some reason, I felt kind of spooked and visually locked in on a security camera that was above the back door. I stared at this red blinking dot on the camera until he opened the door. Suddenly, I let out a sigh of relief as the door closed behind us. We walked to the elevator and rode it to the fifth floor. I repeatedly thought about his remark. I wondered why at that particular moment he would make a comment about me being his woman out of the clear blue sky.

"Everett, if I were not married and I was your woman, you know what I would do right now?" He shook his head, "no," then asked, "What?" I slowly eased up on him, sucked the bottom of his chin, licked his lips, kissed the tip of his nose and slid my hands across his abs. I rubbed my fingers through the fine hairs on his stomach and tenderly groped his nature, which quickly came to attention. It jumped out at me like a mugger and started poking me in my stomach as if it were a weapon. I slowly backed away from him and asked, "Why are you jabbing me in my stomach like that chump?" After no reply, I asked, "What, the cat got your tongue now, Boo?"

He gave me this smirk, which looked as though he thought I might be inviting him to engage in an intimate voyage, but that wasn't the case. From the time we exited the elevator, until we made it to the room, he kept asking me indirect questions to see if that was my intention. I refused to answer, so he blocked the room entrance, once it was open stating,
   "If you want to come in, you better answer my question."
   "MOVE SILLY! Stop blocking the door, or else."
   "Or else what?" He quickly asked.
   "Or else you're gonna get slapped." I repeated in my ruff neck voice.

Now I'm 5'6," 130 pounds; Everett's 6'2, 230 pounds, and I wasn't any kind of match for him at all. He totally ignored me, kept playing and refused to move. I grabbed him around his neck, and we started wrestling. He picked me up, referring to me as, "lightweight," and flipped me over his shoulders. "Now what was all that noise you were talking just a minute ago," he asked, while carrying me into the room and closing the door with his foot. I laughed out loud at him and covered my butt with the back of my hands. I was trying to prevent him from slapping my butt cheeks because I was in a real vulnerable position and I knew he was definitely a rump man.

He plopped me down on a chair in the living area of our suite, sat on the ottoman in front of me with his legs straddled across it and blew me a kiss. He stared at me for a moment with this look, which was actually a look of adoring love. Our eyes seemed to meet at the same time, and I looked away because the moment was deep.

It felt like the perfect moment to capture his undivided attention, so I did just that. "Everett, I really appreciate you and value what we share."

He was modest and tried to convince me that what I was getting from him was nothing special. He swore that no extra efforts were being made on his behalf to woo me or make me think that he was flawless. But, I didn't believe him one bit. I knew that he was on his best behavior and I expressed to him that he could not influence me to think differently.

That night I shared with Everett in detail how disrespected and taken for granted I felt. I told him that my disappointments in Bruce had caused me to become surly and ill-mannered when dealing with men. I used my run-in with Calvin at the detailing shop as an example, and he guaranteed me that I had not become ill-mannered, just tired of dead-end relationships. I guess he could have been half correct, but I never gave it much thought at the time because I truly enjoyed being rude to Calvin that day.

I explained to Everett how I could be all into a man and if provoked, go from charming to bitch in seconds flat. He laughed at my comment, but I informed him that I was quite serious. If he thought I was joking, I advised him that he should not confuse my kindness for weakness.

After all the playing and talking we did, we still had an hour or better to waste. I wanted Everett to hold me, but I didn't have the courage to initiate anything physical between us. I stripped down to my thong and bra, while I prepared for the evening. I strutted from one end of the room to the other, bending to pick up anything and making sure that he was enticed by my every move.

Finally, he must have had a flash back from the elevator, because I looked up and he had reduced his clothing to boxers only. Had I still been buzzing from dinner, I might have been tempted to do a few back bends and leg lifts to provide him with a brief peep show.

But, I wasn't "Bout It" like that, even though I knew I was carrying on like a tease.

He really didn't mind me walking around in my thong. I believe he was somewhat hesitant about moving too fast, out of the respect he established from the first visit. It was evident that he didn't want to make me feel uneasy in any manner, especially since I had finally relaxed with him. However, he was missing all of my nonverbal clues to be close to him, and I was getting frustrated. He obviously didn't realize that I was ready for him to be in my personal space, so he continued to watch television. I didn't know what else to do other than just do the damn thang, but that wasn't me, so out of frustration, I grabbed a pair of slacks and started ironing!

While ironing, I glanced over at Everett. I noticed his look of innocence and was on the verge of screaming, due to temptation. I turned off the iron and crawled into bed with him. He was already aroused and his foreplay immediately introduced itself to me. He kissed, nibbled and sucked, and just as soon as he touched me in the right spot, I knew I had bitten off more than I was ready for. I stopped him in the middle of pulling off my panties, jumped up without ever looking back and went straight into the bathroom. "I'll see you after I get out of the shower," I stated, as I closed the bathroom door and locked it.

My conscience still would not allow me to consummate this relationship and foreplay would be the extent of that intimate encounter. The last thing I remember was seeing him shake his head, as if he were highly disappointed. I don't know if him shaking his head was a sign of disgust, since he was aroused, suited up, and ready for action, or if he was saying, "It's okay, I understand you're nervous." Whatever he was trying to communicate with me wasn't registering. But, I know his eyes were a little sad, and I felt terrible.

"You dummy! This was the perfect opportunity for you to make love to this man and you messed up the entire mood." I thought to myself while showering.

"Damn straight I did. I can't let you come off like easy ass. I needed to assist you in maintaining some kind of self dignity, didn't I?" My conscience asked.

I hung my head in shame, as I thought about all the ways I could have handled the situation differently. I ran shower water in my face to clear my thoughts, bathed and when I felt like I was woman enough to face him again, I turned off the shower and got out.

As I dried myself off, I wondered what his demeanor would be like once I came out of the bathroom. I opened the door and there he was at the sink, brushing his teeth. "Hey sexy! I was missing you," he replied, as he walked up on me and put his arms around my waist. I was so relieved. We were right back on track, as if nothing had ever happened. Those few words were exactly what I needed to hear to feel better about the encounter that occurred between us.

"Kyra, don't worry about what happened earlier, baby. I understand that you're nervous about being with a different man, after so many years of only being with Bruce. But, I will say this; I want to make love to you bad as hell. We're going to go to the club for a few hours, have a few drinks, dance and when we come back to this room, I'm making love to you before we go to sleep."

"Well I guess he told you." I mumbled to my conscience, as he walked into the bathroom.

He may have wanted me sexually that night, but there was absolutely no action after we got in from the club. By the time we returned to the room, we were both exhausted from such a full day. It was all we could do to get undressed for bed. I crawled onto the mattress slower than an aged senior citizen and fell asleep faster than someone under anesthesia.

Everett had to catch an early flight that next morning. By the time we made it to the airport, we only had enough time to hug and say goodbye. I walked him to the checkpoint and watched him as he walked away. I moved over by the window that allowed me to see down the terminal and watched him for as long as he remained in my view. I hoped he would turn around, so that I could wave at him one last time, but he never looked back, and again I left the airport dreading the end of our visit.

I walked to my car repeatedly thinking, "What is it about this man that prevents me from getting him off of my mind for days after he is out of my presence?" There were no answers other than "Him." Meaning the person he was, how he made me feel, and the excitement he added to my life. He gave my life lots of satisfaction, and though I considered terminating the relationship, I had convinced myself to see him once more to be certain that my decision was in fact what I truly wanted.

I arrived home and sat in the living room for hours, watching television in deep thought. Time seemed to move so slowly. It probably was just my imagination, due to the fact that it was also the day that Bruce was scheduled to return home. I occasionally watched the clock, dreading the hour of his arrival. Other than the baby, what would Bruce and I have to talk about? And, how could he even come close to bringing me the same kind of joy I had just experienced with Everett?

Finally, the time for me to pick him up from the airport arrived. I threw on a baseball cap and drove to his sister's house to get Taylor. It took us about twenty minutes to get to the airport. Bruce's plane was landing just as we arrived, so I drove down to the baggage claim door and waited for him to come out.

As we sat there waiting, I started to feel bad about waiting outside for Bruce. "Kyra, you know that's a damn shame. If it were Everett coming into town, you would have arrived early, been looking your best and all up in the airport waiting." However, it wasn't Everett, it was Bruce. If the roles were reversed, he would have done me the exact same way.

I slowly inched up to the main exit and observed people coming and going, loading and unloading, hugging, and kissing. I stopped a few feet from the main door and within a few minutes, Bruce came walking out with his luggage in one hand and a gift for Taylor in the other. I honked the horn and slightly moved forward before he noticed us. When he saw me, he walked in our direction.

"Hi Taylor," He stated in an excited tone, once he was near the car.

"Hi Daddy."

"How's daddy's baby?"

Taylor was so focused on the gift he was holding, she never answered.

"What's that daddy?" She asked, while pointing at the gift in his hand.

"Something for my baby girl."

Bruce handed Taylor her gift and she went at that wrapping paper like a wild child. He put his luggage in the trunk and got into the car.

"Hello Kyra."

"Hey Bruce."

That was the extent of our conversation for the majority of our ride home. Finally, after feeling extremely frustrated with the long silent ride, I blurted out,

"What do you want to do Bruce? Do you want to get a divorce, or what? I can't continue to live like this?"

"Not in front of Taylor, Kyra. I will not have this discussion with you in front of the baby."

"You won't have this discussion period Bruce. I've been trying to make some real sense of this situation for months. Every time I try to address this issue with you, you find a reason not to talk about it with me."

"I will not say one more word about this issue in front of Taylor. I'm telling you now, so if you say anything else to me, I'm going to ignore you."

"Kiss my ass Bruce, you can't ignore me any more than you already have for the past few months. I'm starved for attention and companionship. I'm lonely as hell in my own home and I know marriage should not be this way. I'm tired and if you don't start trying to work out this situation, I'm leaving you. That's a promise."

With as dysfunctional as we already were, that argument was the last thing we needed. Not only did we not speak for the remainder of the ride home, but we also avoided each other for the rest of the week. I walked through the house everyday without saying one word to him. There were times when he didn't even appear to be fazed by my silence, and then there were days when it was clearly obvious that us not speaking bothered him.

I was so out of love with Bruce. My level of compassion for him was minimal. Actually, I could have cared less about his ability to deal with our family problems. I felt like he would have to work through his stressors the best way he could, like I had been doing for so long. I had exhausted all of my patience for Bruce Anthony Murrell. He had failed me as a husband and after weeks of dealing with his lies and selfishness, I was ready to see the man that had become the perfect Band-Aid for all of my personal heartaches.

11

Breaking News

Everett thought I should fly to Detroit to allow him the opportunity to show me his world. I initially suggested that I visit the third week of December, but he informed me that he made plans with his daughters that particular weekend. I didn't want to intrude on their plans, so I suggested a date in January. Right then he informed me for the first time of his breaking news. The first week in January would not be good either because Kimberlin was moving to Detroit. Not only was she moving to Detroit, but she would also be living with him.

I was completely caught off guard and quite surprised when he told me his news. Maybe even more like crushed for a moment, but I quickly recovered. Once I considered my marital status and the fact that I lived over a thousand miles away from him, I couldn't be mad. As he talked, I reflected over our first visit and a conversation we had back in Dallas, regarding Kimberlin. "Aint that a bitch," I kept thinking to myself out of anger. He never lead me to believe when visiting in November that she would be moving to Detroit so soon. Actually, he didn't make it seem as though it was a definite plan at that time at all.

I was quite angry with him after he informed me of her plans to relocate and he could clearly hear it in my voice. I felt very mislead by him regarding their relationship and because of that, I could feel myself pulling back. I could only think, "Save yourself now or deal with the heartaches and consequences of deception later." The intellectual side of me said, "Tell that bitch how betrayed you feel and walk away from this situation right now." But, the emotionally starved side of me encouraged me to think the situation through a little more.

Everett knew he threw me off with the Kimberlin story. Immediately, my attitude was different towards him. The "All in to Bitch," attitude I warned him about during his last visit, went into full effect. He tried not to really acknowledge my mood change, but it was clearly obvious that I was not pleased with him. In order to ease some of the tension brewing between us, he tried to initiate a new conversation. "If I were a genie and could grant you a wish, what would you wish for?" I wasn't up for diverting the conversation, so I never responded to his question. I didn't want to seem desperate, or so deprived for companionship that I settled for or tolerated just anything. I told him, I needed some time to think, and quickly discontinued our conversation.

He called me daily after sharing his news, but I felt it was best that I take some time to myself. After a week of not taking his calls, Everett called the main line to my department at work and Gail answered the phone. She came to my office door and knocked on the window. I motioned for her to come in and she entered with the biggest smile on her face.

"What are you grinning so big for?" I asked, as she approached my desk.

"Girl! Your fine cousin called the main line, and I was lucky enough to answer. He is holding on line two. He told me if I got you on the phone quickly, he would make sure we had dinner together the next time he was in town. You better make sure it happens, too, and don't be hatin on me either."

"What are you talking about Gail? My cousin who, is on the phone?"

"Your cousin Everett is holding on line two."

"Why did he call on your line?"

"He didn't call on my line. He said he called the main number with a family emergency because your line was busy. He's holding on line two. Are you going to get the call or what?"

I was sort of confused about the entire conversation Gail and I were having, so I repeated what she was saying.

"Okay, you said, Everett's on line two with a family emergency? Right!"

"Yeah Kyra, he's on line two. What's wrong with you today girl? You're acting so tripped out lately."

I reached for the phone and noticed Gail still standing in my office. "Thank you Gail, could you please excuse me?" She walked out of my office, shutting the door behind her, and I retrieved his call.

"Kyra Murrell speaking, may I help you?"

"Kyra, why haven't you been taking any of my calls? I've left messages on your cell and office phone everyday for the past week and you haven't returned one of my calls. What's your problem?"

"I think that's rather bold of you to call here and ask me what's my problem like you don't know."

"Ky, I really don't know. What's wrong baby?"

"My problem is you and the fact that you're a damn liar. You haven't been totally honest with me about your relationship. You broke the rules of our affair, which was open communication and honesty, and I'm done."

"I haven't broken any rules, and I have not tried to mislead you. I just didn't know how to tell you about Kimberlin coming because I've fallen in love with you and I didn't want to lose you. I apologize about the way you had to find out and I hope we can work through this."

After our brief discussion, I could only focus on him saying that he loved me. I was shocked at first, and then I considered how stupid I felt for being so vulnerable. I questioned if my self-esteem had become so low, that I'd just fall for anything he told me without doubting him at all.

"Everett when you love someone you're honest with them. I feel like you intentionally mislead me. You should have shared with me during our first visit that Kimberlin was in fact moving. I know you were aware of her plans to definitely relocate, but you only made it

89

seem as though it was a discussion, not an event in motion. I thought we shared a special friendship, but maybe it was more of an adventure or just simply something for you to do until your woman moved to Detroit. I don't know, but whatever the case may have been, I'm hurting behind your actions and I'm through fooling around with you."

"Kyra, please come to Detroit and see me. You are far more to me than a fucking adventure, and you know that. I just need to see you, so that we can talk and try to resolve this."

"There's really nothing for us to resolve. There's nothing else for us to talk about either, and I'm going to go now."

"Wait! Ky, please don't hang up on me."

Right then, I knew I had the upper hand for the moment. I could feel myself allowing the brick wall between us to slowly come down. I believed what he was saying and I wanted to hear him out. I became slightly sensitive to his plea and stumbled upon some compassion for his request for me to stay on the phone.

"Okay, what?" I asked.

"Kyra, just promise me that you will come. We'll talk face-to-face and try to work this situation out."

"Everett, I'll think about coming to Detroit. Give me some time and I'll let you know something in a few days."

"Alright I will. I hope to hear something from you soon. I miss you so much."

"Ok! If you say so," I rudely replied, before hanging up the phone in his face.

I immediately rested my head on my desk. I sighed a few times before massaging my temples in a circular motion. As I lifted my face off of the desk and leaned back in my chair, I noticed Gail peeking through my window. She knocked on the door and once again I motioned for her to come in.

"Kyra! Are you okay? You look terrible."

"I'm fine Gail, thanks for asking."

"Are you sure everything is okay? Because if you need to talk, I'm here."

"Yeah, I'm sure. But thanks for your concern."

Gail left my office holding a stack of files in her arms and returned to her desk. As for me, work was the last thing on my mind, after my conversation with Everett, so I grabbed my belongings and went home for the day.

After about a week, Everett still had not heard from me. He called my office again and wanted to know what I had decided about coming to Detroit. He was determined that he was not taking "no" for an answer. If I decided I would not come there, he assured me that he would make things happen one way or the other. He became irritated with our conversation stating,

"Before you tell me "no" again, I want you to know that if you don't come here, I'll be in Oklahoma this week."

"This week!" I don't know if I'm ready to see you, or if I even want to deal with you any longer. You have violated my trust and I don't know if I should put myself out there to be hurt, just because you say you love me."

"WHAT!!!!!!!! What is it that you want me to say, Kyra? Things are getting way too complex for me. You're really blowing this out of proportion, and I don't understand why you're so mad."

"I'm not blowing a damn thing out of proportion. You should have told me the truth from the beginning Everett."

"I told you the truth, but you're ignoring the truth. You want me to say something that will make it easier for you to just cop out on what we have. Kyra, you have never just been an adventure, or just something for me to do until Kim moved. With all the women here in Detroit looking for a good man, like myself, if I were just looking for an adventure, I could have gotten with any one of these women here in the city. It would have been easier and far cheaper. Kyra, I LOVE YOU! Now deal with that. Like it or not, I'm in love with you and that's the truth."

I listened to his comments, assessed his degree of sincerity and as crazy as I knew it was for me to go to Detroit, I agreed to let him purchase my ticket.

12

On My Way To Detroit

Four weeks after Everett's second visit to Oklahoma, I was on my way to Detroit for our third visit. My plane arrived at Detroit Metro, at eleven o'clock that morning. It was my first time flying since 9-11, so I knew Everett would not be waiting at my gate. I found my way down the extremely long terminal and met him in baggage claim. While looking towards the bottom of the escalator, I noticed him coming out of the men's restroom. I instantly smirked, but I tried to prevent myself from going into a full smile. I was glad to see him; however, I could not be in Detroit acting like all was well. That would have been a mistake on my behalf and it was not my intention to send any mixed messages about my expectations.

In his excitement, he greeted me with the biggest hug. He tried to kiss me, but I turned my face because I still wasn't feeling him like that. He rubbed my back while he held me, but I just couldn't get into him right then. He grabbed my carry on luggage in one hand and tried to hold my free hand with the other. He kept trying to make small conversation, but grew a little frustrated with me when I continued to answer each of his questions with one or two word replies.

Once we arrived at his car, there on the passenger seat sat thirty-six, beautiful, long stemmed, pink and red roses, a chilled bottle of Papaya Juice and a cute little card. I picked up the card and it read, "You walked into my life and stole my heart." His acts of kindness almost caused me to give in, because I discovered that he had been paying close attention to details from some of our initial conversations. We initially spent a lot of time discussing our likes, favorite foods, drinks and qualities we looked for in a mate. I remember mentioning to him in one conversation that I thought long stemmed roses made one of the most beautiful bouquets of flowers. That is why he had them in the car for me and Papaya Juice was simply my favorite drink.

Everett backed out of the parking spot in the airport parking garage and couldn't keep quiet any longer.

"Kyra, I know that you feel disappointed. But, I promise you that I never wanted to do anything to hurt you. I don't know what I have to do to make things right between us again, but I intend to do everything in my power to make you trust me. I love you so much and for the record, you have never been just an adventure. Since day one, I have wished that you could be mine on a full time basis. It is so hard for me to leave you when we're together and I hate hanging up from you after we talk. There are so many nights I lay in bed wishing I could hold you, or just be in your presence. Most of all, I hate that you are going through such trying times with Bruce because I know you deserve better. I can't tell you what to do about your situation. You have to make that decision for yourself. But if I could remove you from that situation, it would have been done long ago."

"Everett, if you feel the way you say you do about me, then why wouldn't you keep our lines of communication open? Did you ever take into consideration how I might feel about this transition that's about to take place in your life? I mean, I realize that I can't stop her from coming, but I think you should have informed me in advance, then allowed me the opportunity to decide if I wanted to continue our relationship or not. You were only thinking about yourself and how you could continue to have your cake and eat it, too, and that was selfish."

"That's not completely true, Kyra."

"Everett, I didn't ask you to comment on if it were true or not. I'm entitled to my opinion and that's what I believe."

"Okay fine. I don't want to argue about this. I know that I have fallen in love with you and I just needed to show you that I really do value you and our relationship."

I opted not to reply after his last statement. I believed him when he said he loved me and it made me defenseless. Besides, Everett had the most desperate look in his eyes while sharing his thoughts with me. He needed for me to believe him and I honestly wanted to. But, my pain and the lack of trust I developed for him prevented me from completely forgiving his behavior. I peeped over at him a few times as he drove to his house. I told myself, "Just let it go and enjoy the weekend." As we pulled up in his driveway, I finally told him that I forgave him and I would try to enjoy myself.

I entered Everett's nicely decorated, three bedroom home through the side door. I walked directly into the kitchen and straight to the master bedroom to put up my bags. As soon as I walked into the room, I noticed twenty helium filled balloons, with curly strings hanging from the ceiling. I smiled as I focused on the balloons to read each one. They read, "You're Special, You're Number One, Welcome, I Miss You," and some were just covered in Happy Faces. He stood in the doorway behind me smiling. I turned towards him and stated,

"This was so thoughtful of you, Everett. Thank you so much."

"You're welcome. I wanted you to know that you are really special to me and I'd never do anything to intentionally hurt you," he replied, as he pulled me in front of him for a hug.

While holding me, he put his mouth next to my ear and whispered, "I'm trying to make it really hard for you to end our relationship." It was already very hard for me to walk away. The special treatment and the surprises he provided for me that day only complicated things for me even more. I could feel myself getting mushy on him, but I was determined not to allow his behavior to distract me.

I suggested that he give me a tour of his lovely home to interrupt the mood. As we walked from room to room, I noticed that it had a woman's touch to it. It wasn't decorated with masculine items as I expected, and no matter how much I wanted to ignore what I was seeing, it certainly flaunted the touch of another woman.

I started reminiscing about our past and thought about us as kids and how unfocused on life Everett was back then. I laughed out loud when I considered how bad he was in school and how he was always in the principal's office for something. It was good to see that he had done so well for himself. I felt extremely proud of his accomplishments. He had beaten the odds and truly done something positive with his life. I never in my wildest dreams would have pictured him and I as an item and here we were, years later, experiencing real heart felt emotions for one another. There was no denying it. I, too, had allowed myself to fall in love. We both knew that our relationship was unhealthy due to the circumstances. But, the purpose of the trip was to come up with some kind of resolution. I was certain that by the time I left Detroit, we would agree on doing what was truly best for us both.

Everett made dinner reservations at Lacey's, which was an upscale restaurant in Troy for that Saturday evening. I wondered if I had ever come off as high maintenance during his visits to Oklahoma because he wanted to take me to a restaurant with sixty-dollar appetizers. I assured him that it wasn't necessary and we could just go get shrimp from one of the Shrimp Shacks or to a Deli for Corn Beef sandwiches. But he refused my suggestion, and insisted that we keep our reservations.

Once we arrived at the restaurant, he valet parked, and I went inside to wait on him. The host took our names and mentioned that they were running about an hour behind schedule on reservations. We decided to wait for a while, but after waiting for over an hour, we canceled our reservation and drove back to Detroit.

"What do you want to do now since our dinner plans were ruined?" He asked.

"We can return to the house, change into something more comfortable and see if Kat wants to go out."

"Call her and see if she wants to go out and drink a few brewskies," he stated while handing me his cell phone.

I called Kat to see what her agenda was looking like for the evening. As usual, she was all for going out that night.

After we changed clothes, Everett stopped by the corner store and purchased a twelve pack of beer and a papaya juice for me. When we arrived at Kat's house, she was already dressed and only needed to put on her make up. Everett opened the case of beer and handed one to Kat and her cousin, Monty. Monty grew up with us as well. He was one of my childhood friends, and hadn't changed much. He was still tall, slinky and silly as ever. He hugged me and immediately started teasing me about still being the oddball. I ended up jokingly telling him off, like old times, and our evening went from there.

"Kyra still talks much shit, don't she Mont?" Kat asked, while walking from her bedroom into the living room sipping on her beer.

"Yeah, she's still a damn trip, sharp as ever with that tongue, but still my girl." He replied while giving me dap.

I didn't mind being the oddball of the group. I had always been, so it was just natural for me to do my thing and feel comfortable with my decision. While we sat around talking, each of them had already drunk three beers apiece, and I was still sipping on the same Papaya juice.

"Kat come on. The club will be closed by the time we get there," I screamed to the back of her apartment.

"Shut up. I'm ready," she responded, while walking to the front. She grabbed her keys, purse, and cell phone, as she drank down the last of her beer, and sat the empty can on the counter.

"Alright, let's do this," Kat stated as she closed her door.

Woody's was packed. It was full to capacity and people were crammed together on the dance floor like sardines. Walking around to mingle wasn't much of an option, but I wasn't really feeling the crowd anyway. The brotha's up in that joint looked major thugged out and the sista's were straight hoochie. All I noticed was ass, tits, slits, and tricks everywhere. "What is up with this place tonight," I thought while looking around with my nose turned up.

Kat's younger sister, Cassandra, had a table in the back of the club, next to the dance floor, so we sat with her and a few of her girlfriends. Everett and Monty stopped by the bar to buy drinks, so they arrived at the table shortly after us. Once Everett sat down, he quickly read my expression. He leaned over and whispered,
"You're uncomfortable in here, aren't you?"
"Yeah, I feel very uncomfortable."
"I should have told you earlier that Saturday nights are packed."
"Yeah, packed with Hoodlums and Hoochies," I replied.
"After Kat and Mont finish their drinks, we'll leave." He responded, while kissing the back of my neck.

Everett got up from his seat, whispered in Kat's ear, and left the table. I figured he told her I was ready to leave. But when I was getting ready to explain why I felt uncomfortable, three of my old classmates approached the table. While talking with them, I heard the DJ announce, "This song is dedicated to that special lady from Oklahoma," our theme song, "What Am I Gonna Do," followed.

I looked across the room for Everett and our eyes seemed to slowly meet at the same time. It was as though we were about to make love for the very first time, and passion filled the air. He was still standing a nice distance away from me. I could see his mouth motioning the words of the song. And though I couldn't hear him singing, I felt the passion he was trying to convey to me. I was blushing and taken by his thoughtfulness. I couldn't give him much eye contact, due to the way I was feeling, but I remember thinking how special it was of him to dedicate a song to me, how special I felt, how gorgeous he was and how honored I was that he worked so hard to keep me in his life.

Kat was the only person who knew Everett and I were seeing each other. Monty looked shocked when the dedication went out. He knew I was married, and assumed that all was well between my husband and me. He didn't say anything to me that night about what was going on, but I know he wanted to.

Everett made me feel like the most fortunate female in the building that evening. I was beaming from my experience with him in just that one day, and I planned to enjoy every bit of the time I had left in Detroit with him. Somehow, he had gone and done it once again. He had found a way to make me feel like his woman, not his mistress and that meant a lot to me. More than anything, he had actually found a way to make me forget that I was ever angry with him.

After my dedication, I still wasn't feeling the crowd in the club that night. We decided to leave Woody's and go downtown to the Motor City Casino. Mitch, one of our classmates and Everett's best friend, was in the club that night and was trying his best to get with Kat. She shared with me her interest in him and the fact that she had warned him not to play mind games with her because she would sleep with a married man. That was right up Mitch's alley. Actually, it was just what he wanted to hear because realistically, although he was married, he, too, participated in extra marital affairs. Kat had given Mitch the verbal confirmation he was looking for regarding them, and from that point on, he was after her.

Kat had Mitch's nose wide open that night; so he decided to accompany us to the Casino. Everett and the fellas played the card tables, while Kat and I played the slot machines. After being in the Casino for over two hours and losing lots of money, everyone was hungry. Kat rode with Mitch in his Hummer, and Everett and I followed them to Mildred's Café on Seven Mile. We sat around in the restaurant, having breakfast, laughing, talking loud and trying to keep the morning young. It seemed real odd for us to be having such great fun after years of no contact, but we managed to pull it off and were carrying on like we were still in middle school.

I was so intrigued with Everett after leaving the casino. The way he looked at me was much different than before. I believe we became noticeably confused after he dedicated that song to me. Several times throughout the night, I glanced over at him, and he appeared to be in deep thought. My mind was no longer focused on the group discussion I was having with everyone else. Instead, I focused on him and questioned what he might be thinking. "Could it be that he was in love with two women at the same time?" I kept asking myself. That question seemed to play over and over in my mind, and I kept coming up with the same answer. I didn't believe that he would allow himself to truly fall in love with both of us, but he knew that I was no longer in love with Bruce, so maybe it was possible.

Everett knew why I remained with Bruce, so he knew that Bruce was of no real threat to him. But I realized that Kimberlin's moving in with him would clearly complicate our relationship. He seemed to ignore the fact that her living with him on a full-time basis would change his life significantly.

His look during breakfast appeared to be a glazed stare of infatuation and newfound happiness. Passion could be seen in his eyes, and it was clearly obvious that we had to work through some issues before my visit was over. While we sat at the table looking puzzled, Mitch and Kat walked over to the cash register to pay their tab and left. Seconds later, we followed.

Everett didn't live too far from the restaurant, so we arrived at his place rather quickly. Once we made it to the house, he set the alarm and we settled in. Mother nature popped in on me with an early-unannounced visit. Any plans of intimacy he might have made prior to my arrival, were surely blown out of the water. "I guess God is trying to tell us something," I said, while closing the bathroom door to take a shower.

Sunday morning brought about new adventures. I had a new attitude, and my mind was set on handling business. Everett was going to discuss Kimberlin with me before we did anything and that was not an option. I was under lots of pressure and needed to talk with him about the issues that concerned me most about our relationship. I sat on the arm of the couch in his bedroom and expressed my concerns.

"Everett, I feel like we need to have a long overdue conversation about you, Kimberlin, her moving here and myself. When I mentioned her in the past, you have changed the subject to avoid any real detailed dialogue about her. I'm not going to allow that to happen today. We are going to talk about our situation whether you want to or not."

He knew from the tone in my voice that there was no way he could avoid having this discussion. He pulled me into the living room and turned off his cell phone. I sat on the couch, and he provided me with his undivided attention. I took a few deep breaths to relax and then proceeded with our discussion.

"I know that you and Kim have been together for ten months. I hate that I met you after your relationship started to blossom with her because I'm really not dogmatic like that. I want to respect her as a woman and do what I know is right. I believe the relationship you two are trying to establish is important to you or you wouldn't be moving her here. You are such a wonderful guy, Everett, so I clearly understand why Kim is moving here to be closer to you. However, in order for you to give her one hundred percent of what she deserves and one hundred percent of your time, I feel like I need to totally remove myself from the equation. You need time to see if your relationship with her is what you truly desire for yourself without me running interference."

Everett listened as I spoke with his right index finger curved above his top lip. But, what I was saying just wasn't registering. He wasn't trying to agree with me, and for every reason I suggested that we end our relationship, he provided a reason it needed to continue. He had all the correct answers, and said everything I wanted to hear. But isn't that just like a man who's been given the opportunity to live in the glory of having his cake and eating it, too.

"Kyra, I can maintain this relationship. If you just give me a chance, I'll show you that I can. Kimberlin is moving here, but I don't even know if that's what I want for myself. I asked her to move here long before I fell in love with you. After my feelings for you started to develop, it was too late. Kim had already given her notice and was making plans to move. I won't disappoint you and that's a promise. I have every intention on making it virtually impossible for you to just walk out of my life, and I'm not going to let you give up on me just like that. I've always been a go-getter baby, and I want you in my life. This relationship between us can work, and what you really need to know is that if I want to see you bad enough, I'll fly out of Detroit first thing in the morning and return that same night. I can't deny it Kyra, I have fallen hard for you, and for my own selfish reasons, I always want you to be a part of my life."

Bouts of confusion started to consume my thought process. It was obvious that no real solutions had been confirmed. My head started to hurt from just thinking and talking about our circumstances. I decided not to press the issue anymore that day or for the remainder of my visit. I just decided it wasn't worth the stress and tried to enjoy the duration of my stay.

I had business I needed to tend to back in Oklahoma, so I changed my departure time. That Tuesday, Everett dropped me off at the airport on his way to work. We pulled up in front of the airport at five-thirty in the morning. I kissed him goodbye, grabbed the handle of my luggage, and entered the double doors of the airport. Not once did I look back because my mind was finally at rest. I had this feeling of peace as I approached the ticket counter to check in. I didn't understand what was going on with me emotionally. However, I knew I no longer felt insecure about Kimberlin.

After learning more about her from Everett over the weekend, I believed that I was quite unique to him in my own way. I didn't leave Detroit with all of the answers I was hoping to acquire from my visit, but I was leaving with more than I initially arrived with in regards to his significant other. One thing I realized was that if Everett didn't know anything else, he knew Kimberlin was out of my league by far, which I believe is why he always tried to evade some of my questions about her.

Her intent to move, however, was made crystal clear for me when I noticed her furniture had already been shipped from Chicago. It was stored in a corner in Everett's basement, and I noticed it while touring his home on the Saturday I arrived. I realized that day that he undoubtedly knew she was moving to Detroit during his first visit to Oklahoma. I suppose he thought he would just enjoy my company until she was there on a full-time basis, and slowly fade out of my life once she arrived. He never thought he would fall in love with me, and that's where he played himself.

I believe that we were both surprised to experience what we found in each other, once we became close. But, I had always been honest with him about my situation, and I wished he had done the same. I realize that it was too late for regrets; I allowed myself to fall for him and it was up to me to work this situation out for myself. As I sat at the gate waiting to board my plane, I grew a little angry at the thought of just being someone for him to pass time with. Then, I considered the fact that I really shouldn't be angry because again I willingly allowed the situation to happen.

Had my affair not taken place, I might have had a nervous breakdown from the stress of my marital situation. Everett was an outlet for me, and he knew that. I openly expressed that fact to him when we started getting close. So, although I had grown very attached to him, he always knew the real purpose he served in my life.

I lined up to board my plane and instantly started thinking about Mr. Barnett. I captured thoughts of his beautiful smile and all of the special memories he and I shared since we had been seeing each other. There were so many great times that replayed in my mind. I found myself laughing a few times out loud when I thought about his busy hands and how sassy he was during our first night together. I could never stop thinking about his sexy lips kissing mine whenever we were in an elevator. That had actually become one of my most cherished memories of him. In continuing my thoughts of us, I concluded that my trip to see him was well worth the journey.

The thought of what we could have been came to mind and made my heart ache a little. I had always told Everett before ending a phone conversation to, "Never Settle," and here I was expecting him to compromise his morality to have an affair with me, not to mention that I was doing the same. I just couldn't impose on his happiness and his desire to be in a stable relationship any longer. I could see that allowing him to continue to spend intimate time with me was for my own selfish reasons, as well. It wasn't right for me to infringe upon Kimberlin's happy home just because my house was a mess. I knew I had to stop seeing him out of respect for myself because at this point, I was no better than the woman that I assumed was having an affair with Bruce. The more I thought about my actions, the worse I felt, and I became overwhelmed with guilt, while standing in line. Finally, the desk attendant called for boarding in rows six through ten. As I boarded my plane and buckled myself in, thoughts of Mr. Barnett and myself came to an end.

13

Reality & Struggles

Weeks passed and I was trying to get my life back in order and feeling my way with Bruce. The connection between us was awful, and divorce court was looking more and more like a reality. Our conversation around the house was still limited, and we were so distant that having any kind of sensible dialogue was impossible. At this point conversations about Taylor didn't even go well for us. We clearly disliked each other, and even if my trips brought about temporary peace, coming home was always a reminder of the mental hell I was going through.

Bruce found pleasure in being away from home as well. When he was in town, he continued to stay away from home as late as he could without my killing him. When he was home, no family bonding went on between us. We often found ourselves relaxing in different areas of the house, and we never sat around each other for any significant amount of time because an argument was sure to follow. Neither of us had any kind of patience for the other. He was extremely short with me, and I was just as short with him. Anything and everything he attempted to do to make our situation better got on my nerves. I was trying to adjust to life without Everett, which was extremely hard for me. There were moments when I wanted to speak with him just to hear his soothing voice, but I didn't call because we were moving on with our separate lives.

The Christmas holiday was quickly approaching. There was certainly nothing-festive going on in the Murrell household for the holiday season. Bruce and I shopped separately for Taylor, never bothering to discuss with each other the gifts we purchased for her. We separately wrapped our gifts, which prevented us from knowing if Taylor would have duplicate gifts on Christmas morning, and it was evident that neither of us really cared. Our poor baby was suffering to some extent already from the struggles of our dysfunctional marriage. Here Bruce and I were supposed to be preparing to celebrate a holiday with our only child, and neither of us was carrying on like we were a family who loved one another.

After several weeks of not speaking with Everett, I decided to call him to say hello. He had always been good to talk to when I was feeling a little stressed out, which is why I often struggled to end our relationship. When I called, I was expecting the warm greeting I always received. But when he answered his phone, he was short and informed me that he was visiting with his ex-girlfriend's sister. I noticed that he wasn't himself, which caused me to become irritated. I was trying to understand his demeanor, but the conclusion I came up with for his behavior was not good. Either he was still seeing his ex-girlfriend or he was seeing her sister. My suspicions made me more irritated, which caused me to abruptly end our conversation. "Just who does this bitch think he's dealing with?" I asked myself after hanging up.

The more I thought about his behavior throughout the night, the madder I became. I didn't rest well that evening and I couldn't wait until the next morning. I wanted to call Everett so I could give him a piece of my mind, but I knew I had to get myself together. I also remembered that my relationship with him was only supposed to be a friendly one. But to be honest, it was difficult to just, "Get Myself Together." Hell! My heart was involved.

That following morning, he called my office, but I missed his call and refused to call him back. I figured when he finally realized that I would not be returning his call, he'd call back when he was ready to talk again and my speculations were correct. Shortly after noon, my phone rang once again, and I answered,

"International Affairs, Mrs. Murrell speaking, how may I help you?"

"Hey baby, what are you doing?"

"No he isn't acting like we're on good terms," I thought as I replied in the driest tone I could find within. "Not too much Mr. Barnett."

My response alone was cold enough for Everett to realize that I was in fact pissed off with him. There was no need for him to guess my mood because I wasn't sugar coating anything at all.

"I've been calling you all morning, Kyra. Where have you been?"

"I've been right here in my office, sitting at my desk all day. First I missed your call, and the last time you called, I just simply didn't feel like talking to you, so I didn't answer my phone."

"Why are you not taking my calls? I kind of sensed that you were upset with me last night when you hung up. It just never dawned on me to call right back to inquire about what was wrong."

"I'm sure it didn't since you were pre-occupied."

" Well, I guess I should ask what you're mad about?"

"What I'm mad about?" I repeated.

I felt like talking real ignorant to him, when he said, "I guess I should ask what you are upset about." I was convinced that he had slipped on something, bumped his head and lost his mind. Without wasting another second of my time or his, I just went there.

"What do you mean you guess you should ask? There's nothing to guess. You should most certainly ask, if you don't know. I don't normally just get upset with you and hang up like I did last night, so you should have known that there was some kind of problem and called back."

"You're right, I apologize, I should have called back."

I expressed to Everett how angry I was with the manner in which he interacted with me on the phone, while visiting his ex-girlfriend's sister. My concern was not the fact that he was visiting her, but the tone in which he used while talking with me. There appeared to be more to their relationship than he initially shared.

And though I had been carrying on like a damn fool for the past few months, he needed to recognize that I in fact, was not one.

He said that he was under a lot of stress and not happy about my decision about our relationship. I apologized for possibly over reacting, but shared with him that I too was going through withdrawals as well. However, my mind was made up, and I was going to stick with my decision to pull out of the relationship no matter how hard things became at home. When we hung up that afternoon, we were both fully aware of the struggles the other was experiencing due to the sudden changes between us.

Christmas morning arrived. Bruce and I sat in the den with Taylor, as she opened her gifts. There were a few gifts under the tree that I purchased for him from her. But in spite of our differences, he wasn't smart enough to do the same for me. I handed him his gifts with a smirk on my face that said, "Yeah asshole, I know you didn't get me anything." I was determined that I would be the bigger parent, and I could see the distress in his face. It was all I could do to converse with him, as he tried to assure me that he didn't know what to get a woman who already had everything. He wrote me a check for two thousand dollars to buy whatever I wanted, which wasn't necessary. The damage was already done, and I had my own darn money. I was furious and briefly considered starting an argument, but our home had been so pleasant that day, and I didn't want to spoil Christmas for Taylor, so I let it go.

Opening gifts that morning was the most excitement we had experienced in our home in some time. I don't know if we found it in ourselves to get along because it was the Lord's Day, or because it was our daughter's first real Christmas. Whatever the case may have been, it was a pleasant experience, and we tried to make sure that the day ended on that same note.

As Christmas came to a close, I know I must have thought about Everett a zillion times. I wondered how the holiday had gone with him and Kimberlin. It really bothered me that I wasn't able to talk with him for the holiday, and it bothered me even more when I thought about his decision to move her to Michigan. For his sake, I hoped that all was going well between the two of them because his decision to move her to Detroit right before Christmas wasn't working for me at all. I wondered if I had made the right decision to no longer see him; then my conscience rattled off, "Kimberlin would have caused major interference. Don't second guess yourself; you made the right decision." If I made the right decision, I sure didn't feel like I had.

A few days after Christmas, I got a call from Herbert Perkins, the CEO of Perkins Enterprise. He called to confirm what would, in time, turn out to be my biggest nightmare. Bruce was having an affair. I immediately started crying and asked the investigator if he was sure. He assured me that he had enough photos of Bruce and his mistress to cover a gymnasium floor and wanted to deliver them to me. I informed him that I would pick them up later in the week because I simply wasn't ready to deal with the hard facts now that they had unfolded. I felt like kicking Bruce's ass for the pain he was causing me. I mean, I really wanted to do some serious bodily harm to that man. But how would it benefit me to hurt him so bad that I put Taylor in the position of not getting to know her father.

New Year's was a tearful holiday for me. I spent most of the day alone. Taylor had gone with Bruce to his parents' house for dinner, and I stayed home sitting around like a zombie. I didn't realize that confirming Bruce's affair would hurt as much as it did. Finding out the truth seemed to hurt worse than not knowing at all. I guess when I didn't know for a fact about his affair, I, at least, had the satisfaction of only assuming. Realistically, I didn't know if I could handle the news of Bruce's affair, but it caused me to become even more withdrawn and extremely bitter. For the days that followed, I tried to find activities to do that would keep me occupied, but the more I tried to find to keep myself busy, the harder it became.

Bruce was home for the remainder of the holiday break, and the activities he planned never included me. Not once did I mention to him that I had evidence to prove his infidelity, and I didn't know exactly when I might mention that I was aware of it either. I considered not saying anything at all in order to build my case for a divorce. But I didn't know if it was realistically possible for me to hold something of that magnitude for that long, though I was going to try.

The last days of my vacation seemed to creep by at first, but as I found activities to do and friends to socialize with, time moved a little faster. Though my situation didn't look good, I was trying to feel confident about the changes that were occurring in my life. I had been Everett free for about fifteen days, which was a major accomplishment for me. The Sunday before I was to return to work, I was slightly anxious to get back to my professional routine. I thought returning to work might add some stability to my life, which would help keep my mind occupied with something besides my personal troubles.

Monday morning, the first working day of 2002, I pulled into my reserved parking space at work feeling energized. I stepped out of my car looking like a million bucks, walked into the building, rode the elevator to the seventh floor, spoke to everyone as I walked to my office, sat down at my desk, and cried like a two-year old. Here I was back at work in 2002 and nothing had changed. I reached across my desk for a tissue to wipe my eyes and there was Gail standing in my doorway. She was all prepared to tell me about her holiday vacation, but became alarmed by my tears.

"Kyra, are you alright?"
"Yes, thank you for asking. I'm just having a bad day." I replied, while dabbing my eyes dry.
"Well do you want to talk to someone about what's going on."
Just as I was about to share my heartaches with Gail, my office phone buzzed.

"International Affairs, Kyra speaking."
"I LOVE YOU!"

"Excuse me," I quickly replied.

"Hey Ky, it's me, Everett."

"Hi Everett," I mumbled before bursting into tears on him.

"Baby, what's wrong?"

I covered the mouthpiece of the phone and asked Gail to excuse herself, while I talked on the phone. As she exited, I stated,

"Ok, I'm back."

"What's wrong, why are you crying?"

"Bruce is having an affair."

"How do you know; what makes you say that?"

"Over the holiday break the Private Investigator I hired called and told me."

"Damn! That son of a bitch! Baby, I'm sorry. Do you need me to come down there?"

"And do what? There's nothing you can do about this, Everett."

"Hold you. I can hold you and kiss away your tears. That's all I want to do. Kyra, I miss you, and if I can be with you at a time like this to console you, that's what I want to do."

I was on a "pity party" from that point on. After that, he wasn't able to make much sense of anything I was saying, due to my crying. He listened for a few minutes and tried to talk me into calming down, but I wouldn't respond. Finally, he told me that he was calling his travel agent to have her book him a reservation. "I'll call you back with details later on this afternoon. I love you and please stop crying before you give yourself a headache or make yourself sick." He hung up the phone, and Gail tried to come back into my office to console me, but by then I didn't feel much like talking. I thanked her for being concerned, and she went back to her office.

As usual, talking with Everett made me feel a little better. Him saying how much he missed me stood out most in my mind and made me happy. I didn't think that his new live-in sweetheart would approve of him taking a solo trip so soon, nor did I think that it was a good idea for us to see one another. But my feelings for him were still very strong, and I wanted to see him so badly. I realized that us seeing each other might not be in our best interest and would surely be a setback for me. But I needed to be held, and if he was able to work out a trip, I wasn't going to fight with him about making it happen.

That Monday afternoon, Everett called back just like he said he would.

"Kyra, you need to come up with some kind of story for Bruce. I just purchased us tickets to Kansas City for the weekend."

"What! Kansas City! Why Kansas City?"

"Because it was centrally located, and every other city I had my agent check was over a thousand dollars for each of us."

"What about Kimberlin. She's not going to let you leave this soon on a trip by yourself, is she?"

"Let me deal with Kimberlin. I'm the man of my house, so stop worrying about her because I'm not."

"How do you know I'm free for the weekend?" I asked.

"You're not, you're meeting me in Kansas City, so pack your bags, make an appointment to get your hair done, then find something sexy in that closet of yours for me, and I'll see you Friday."

14

Be Careful What You Encourage

I called Kat to inform her of Bruce's affair and my decision to meet Everett in Kansas City. "What are you going to do for Everett this time?" Kat asked. I really hadn't given it much thought and asked her if she had any suggestions. She thought since we had been doing Genie themes, a message in a bottle would be cute.

My depressed state of mind almost instantly improved after I told Bruce I was going away on business. I could tell he became concerned with my behavior and wondered why there was a sudden change in my demeanor, after days of dragging around. Concerned or not, he never bothered to ask what was going on with me, and I never bothered to tell him. I was tired of fighting, tired of worrying about who his other woman was and overjoyed because I was going to have a mental break from my stressful situation.

Although things were terrible between Bruce and I, I still hoped that he would provide me with a reason to cancel my trip. But, as always, Bruce was Bruce. I was beginning to accept the fact that we were two very different people who had simply grown apart. Out of respect for my daughter, I felt it was necessary to give him my reservation information in case of an emergency. I thought he might get a little suspicious about my leaving because my plans were so last minute. But he was nonchalant about my trip and sarcastically encouraged me to have a great time. "Just like Bruce," I thought and decided that it was quite useless to waste my time with hopeless wishes where our failing marriage was concerned. "Be careful what you ask for, you just might get it," became my motivational slogan for the rest of the week. Since Bruce told me to have a nice time, I planned on doing just that once I arrived in Kansas.

Thursday, the day before my trip to Kansas City, Kat called me from her cell phone. It was extremely late because I was already in bed, and she was very upset about something. At first I couldn't make out what she was saying, but it finally registered.

"Kyra! Everett came up in Woody's tonight with Kimberlin."
"Are you serious Kat?" I asked.
"Hell yeah, I'm serious and I don't like that bitch. She's a short, snooty, ugly, long nose tramp."

I tried to understand why she was so angry with Everett for bringing Kimberlin to the club. Kat was friendly with everyone and rarely met a stranger she couldn't converse with. Finally, she explained that Everett introduced her to Kimberlin and Kimberlin was rude to her in return. When Everett and Kim initially came into the club, he stopped by Kat's seat, hugged her, briefly chatted with her and her sister, and then walked off. He neglected to introduce Kimberlin to them at that time, which made her angry and the situation escalated from there.

"Kat, I can't believe that happened. Everett said Kimberlin was really a nice girl. I bet she became defensive because she thought he was probably trying to talk to you and that's why he didn't introduce her."
"Kyra, that girl is far from being nice. She better be glad I didn't rock that jaw of hers for acting like a bitch. I don't even know what he sees in that non-dressing tramp. She wears a ton of makeup, was dressed bold as hell and not near as classy as you. She isn't his type of woman. Everett was just lonely and done settled for a low budget, broke, mean ass, trick. What he needs to do is send that tramp back to Chi-Town where he found her grimy ass."

I zoned out on Kat while she was talking for a second. She had given a sista the confirmation I needed about Ms. Kimberlin. She said all the key words, which were like music to my ears... "Ugly, snooty, unfriendly, classless, jealous and grimy." With words like that, I knew Everett was coming to Kansas City without any static from home. After listening to Kat, my conclusion of their relationship was that Kimberlin met Everett and saw a bus ticket out of the ghetto. But, his relationship wasn't for Kat or me to judge; we just needed to be prepared to provide support, if his relationship didn't go as planned.

Kat was about to say something, but I cut her off and stated,

"Girl, after I saw Kimberlin's furniture sitting in Everett's basement, I knew in December that we weren't on the same level. But, Everett has found some kind of satisfaction in her or she wouldn't be living with him."

"That's fine Ky. If he likes it, I love it for him, but it's about respect. If Kimberlin was upset with Everett, she should have waited until they were alone instead of embarrassing him in front of his friends. Everett's woman is an insecure ass bag lady. I don't care what he said she was, she has moved here on some old shit. A brotha from her past, dogged her out and she is taking it out on him."

"Calm down Kat. She probably just felt like he spent too much time talking to you before he introduced you to her."

"I don't like her, and he needs to send her ass back to Chicago where she came from with all that bullshit. She was seconds from getting popped in her damn mouth. She better be glad Everett is my boy or he would have been pulling my foot out of her ass."

"Where is he right now and what did he say about the way she talked to you?" I asked.

"He's down at the other end of the bar looking down here at me while I'm talking to you. I told him that I was about to call you and tell you about his bitch. And for the record, his punk ass ain't say one damn word when she was being rude to me. He just stood there looking just as shocked as I was."

"Kat, you should have told, Kim, bitch, it ain't me that your man is spending major chips on and flying all around the damn world to see. It's my girl," I cynically stated, while laughing.

We both laughed, and then I discontinued our conversation because the more questions I asked, the madder she got. When she finally calmed down, I told her to try and have a good time. I also told her to call me when she made it home. I hung up with Kat feeling a little bad for Everett for a moment; then I thought, "That's what his punk ass get for moving that, message taking, pen pushing, gold digger up there to begin with."

Kat didn't call back that night, but bright and early the next morning, Everett did. I could hear the stress in his voice when he asked,

"Hey Kyra, how are you this morning?"

"I'm doing great and what about you?" I cheerfully replied.

"I had a bold experience at Woody's with Kimberlin last night. Have you talked to Kat?"

"Yeah, she told me about your woman clowning at the club last night. She also told me that she didn't like that bitch."

I knew I shouldn't have repeated the fact that Kat called his girl a "bitch," but I found pleasure in rubbing his nose in his public embarrassment, so I did.

"Yeah she was real rude to Kat in the club last night for some reason. I don't even know where that came from. I was so embarrassed, but glad that Kat handled herself like a woman because you know how ghetto she can get."

"You sound like you're a little stressed about the incident."

"No! I'm more like mad as hell because I've never seen Kim act like that before."

I really didn't know what Everett wanted me to say, nor did I know if I desired to say anything on Kimberlin's behalf at all. I just tried to listen and be as supportive as I possibly could. All I could offer him was a listening ear because I certainly couldn't be her cheerleader. I made up my mind long before Kat called that night that I wasn't ever going to interject my opinion about his relationship with Kimberlin. There was no way I would ever sound like a hater when it came to her.

I said very little while he talked about his situation, and once I grew tired of hearing about her, I assured him that I had confidence in his ability to make the best decision for the both of them and then changed the subject.

"Is there anything special you want to do while we're in Kansas City?" I asked.

"Nothing, other than spend some quality time with my baby."

"Oh! So now I'm your baby since your ghetto-licious girlfriend got you out and embarrassed your butt in public."

"Ha, ha, ha. I see you got jokes today. Well, we'll see who's laughing later on tonight."

"Yeah we will. I'll see you later."

"Ok, make sure you're ready to stay up late, because we're hanging." He replied.

Hours before my trip, I ran around as usual trying to locate all of the materials needed for my message in a bottle. I went from one side of town to the next looking for a shapely bottle because all genies had one. I needed to find a bag of red glitter, which would be used to set off the illusion of a genie sprinkling pixie dust when I presented his gifts.

I found a pocket size Tasmanian devil photo album, which I filled with photos of myself, and I also purchased some colorful handprint stickers. The stickers would constantly remind him of the nickname I had given him during our first visit. I grabbed some solar system confetti that symbolized the level of happiness I experienced when we were together. The balloon confetti represented the balloons he gave me during my visit to Detroit. Each color communicated a message I wanted to share with him about my perception of our relationship. The purple balloon represented his being a man of quality; gold represented his value to me; blue represented the altitude we frequently traveled to be together; green represented the money spent to make our relationship the success it had been, and pink simply represented his feminine side, which he was definitely in touch with.

I wanted everything I put in his Genie bottle to convey some type of message about the times we shared together. While I was standing in the checkout line, I saw some M&M's on the rack and threw them in strictly for the slogan, "Melt In Your Mouth, Not In Your Hands," which is exactly what I planned to do, once we finally settled in and started spending some quality time alone.

"Everett's going to really love this surprise," I thought, as I envisioned him reading the scrolled note in his bottle. He was the type who was so easy to please and extremely appreciative of the simplest gifts, which was one of his greatest qualities. And with all of the thought and time that had gone into pulling it together, I was sure he would at least appreciate my creativity and not view my gift as corny.

I picked up a hand full of cards that consisted of topics we often communicated about when we talked on the phone. I use to always send him cards, but stopped right before Kimberlin moved in with him. So, I was determined that he would receive one last card from me, which was sure to stay on his mind when he returned home.

One of the cards had a picture of a bottle lying on a beach, with a scrolled message in it. This was the perfect card to initiate the illusion I was trying to establish and the one I decided to give him first. My shopping spree took me to the Jake's Corner Store to buy a box of condoms, which caused me to feel a little embarrassed considering I was not buying them to use with my husband.

I knew long before leaving Oklahoma that I was going to make love to Everett in Kansas City. We were long overdue, and my curiosity had gotten the best of me. Besides, Everett knew that I highly promoted safe sex, so I was certain that he was going to arrive with condoms for the occasion, as well. I had no intentions of letting him know that I bought condoms. I only purchased them to ensure that we had enough protection to last the entire weekend.

Finally, I made it to the last store and purchased a tarnished ring, which would symbolize our vow to remain friends, a cork, which would go on the top of the bottle to seal our bond and finally a Sean John jean outfit, with a baby blue turtleneck sweater. When I arrived home, I paced in and out of the house a few times trying to sneak in the items I had purchased. Bruce was in his office and kept getting out of his chair. He walked into the bedroom to see what I was doing a few times, but never said a word. I could see in his expression that he wondered just what I was doing, but instead of asking, it was easier to disregard my behavior.

He usually ignored me for the sake of maintaining his own sanity. He looked at me a few times with his typical, stupid, Bruce expression on his face, but, again, never asked me one question. Since he didn't care enough to ask, I didn't care enough to tell. I just gave him a stupid look in return and walked out of the bedroom. I pulled my luggage out of the closet and started packing. While packing, I smiled repeatedly, as I thought about making love to Everett for the first time.

Before leaving the house, I made sure I wrote down all of my flight information and my hotel number. I put it on the kitchen counter and grabbed my bags. "I'll see you Sunday Bruce," I yelled, while walking out the door, and once it was closed, I mumbled, "You said have a great time, but you better be careful about what you encourage me to do because I just might do it Bruce. **I JUST MIGHT DO IT!"**

15

Kansas City

Prior to driving to the airport, I stopped and bought him a bottle of Cognac. Before I checked my bags, I slid the bottle in the front pocket of my luggage, and then put it on the scale.

"Has your luggage been out of your possession at any time Mrs. Murrell?" The airport attendant asked.

"No."

"Well, has anyone asked you to carry on a bag for them?"

"No."

"Great! Your seat is F-8 and you will board at gate B-2 on the 4:45 flight to Kansas City."

"Thank you," I replied as I grabbed my ticket and walked to the terminal.

Once I made it to the security checkpoint, I threw my purse and Everett's oversized teddy bear gift bag on the belt for a security check. As I walked through the scanner the alarm went off. "DANG, that alarm would go off on me," I mumbled while shaking my head.

"Ms., can you step to the side to be searched?" An officer asked.

"Sure, no problem," I replied

"I need a female security officer with a hand wand to check this woman," the male officer yelled, as I moved over to the side to be searched.

"Ms. we're going to need you to take off your boots," the female officer stated.

"My boots?"

"Yes! We need to scan your boots for explosives."

"Do you mind if I get my bags off the belt first. I don't want someone to walk away with my things?"

"Sure you may get your things as soon as you hand me your boots."

As I approached the table to retrieve my bags, a gentleman asked if he could search my luggage at a nearby table. Something in my bag alarmed the screening agents while they were scanning my luggage. Finally, after an in-depth search, security told me I was free to go, but I had to leave a nail file that was in my purse because the metal tip on it could be used as a weapon. "Sure sir, that's fine," I stated while smiling.

When I arrived at my gate, the three o'clock flight was backing away to leave. Right after the plane departed from the gate, a utility truck caught on fire causing a major disturbance. Emergency vehicles came from everywhere. My smile fell from my face as it registered in my mind that this incident would surely delay my flight from leaving on time. I immediately became antsy. While bouncing my leg like a six year old, I looked out of the window. I wondered if they would remove the smoking truck before my plane arrived. I kept looking at my watch, but that didn't seem to make time pass any faster. It took forever for them to get the smoking truck under control. When it was removed the arriving plane pulled in, and I was allowed to board my plane. My flight departed twenty-five minutes later than the scheduled time, but at least we departed.

Once we were off the ground, I relaxed. I grabbed the American Way Magazine from the back of the chair next to me and scanned through it. I made it as far as page eighty and found myself laughing, as I read my horoscope, which read, "New experiences in your life will bring about great happiness. Enjoy them all, but be prepared to STAND when changes knock at your door." Everett's horoscope read, "Since all the secret affairs you are currently conducting are taking place in out-of-the-way locations, you're probably safe to continue carrying on as furtively as you have been. (You're not above such things.) The deals made behind closed doors may be dangerous, but they sure are exciting. So, if you're not misbehaving by now, shame on you."

DAMN!!!!!!!!!! Was his horoscope an indirect approval from Satan himself, or was I just tripping out? I didn't know what to think, and I didn't want to think about what to think for too long. I didn't want anything to spoil my weekend, so I simply turned the page and continued to scan the magazine.

My flight was originally due to arrive in Kansas City at five fifty-two. However, I arrived at my gate about five minutes late. I knew Everett would be waiting for me at my gate because his plane was scheduled to get in fifteen minutes before mine. We initially discussed his meeting me at my gate and going from there to Baggage Claim together. But when I de-boarded my plane and entered the airport, I looked all over, and there was no Everett. "Man I know he didn't go to baggage claim without me," I mumbled while lifting his gift bag to my shoulder. I walked down to glance at the flight monitors and discovered that his plane was just arriving a few gates away. I walked to his gate and propped my back up against a phone booth, while I waited for him to de-board his plane.

As I watched for Everett, I noticed two tall gentlemen entering the airport and right behind them he followed. He was so engaged in a conversation with a woman he flew in with that he didn't realize I was there until after she put a small piece of paper in his hand. When we made eye contact, I could tell that he wasn't quite sure if I saw him accept the paper or not. Instead of getting angry, I gave him this look, like busted and cunningly smirked at him.

"Hey baby," he said while pulling me closer for a kiss.
"Hey." I replied, while smoothing out my lip-gloss.
"Have you been waiting here long?"
"No, I just arrived myself."
"All I kept thinking about, while flying in was that you were going to be mad at me because my plane was late."

"Well you're wrong. How am I going be mad at you about something you had absolutely no control over? By the time I de-boarded my plane, it was six o'clock. I immediately checked the monitors after I discovered you weren't waiting for me and headed to this gate. When I arrived, people were already coming off the plane, so actually I didn't wait very long for you at all."

"What's that?" He asked, while pointing at the bag I was holding.

"This is for you." He took the gift bag I was holding and instantly grabbed my free hand.

We walked through the terminal to baggage claim making small talk about our flights. Once we made it to our location, we questioned the service attendant about which of the four carousels our luggage would be on. The luggage from both flights was scheduled to come in on carousel A or B, which were located right next to each other. Everett and I stood between the two carousels and talked, while waiting for our flight numbers to pop up on the digital monitor. We had been talking for some time when I realized that neither of our flight numbers had shown up. I had grown slightly impatient, so I walked back over to the information counter and asked the attendant to check the baggage roster once again. Just as I was returning to my spot between the carousels, Everett's flight number popped up on the monitor for carousel A.

We watched some of the same luggage go around forever, and finally, his luggage came around. My luggage had still not shown up. We walked over to carousel C just to check for my bag before reporting it lost, and there it was, lying on its side. I grabbed my bag and walked through security looking for auto rentals. Rent-A-Car, car rental was right next to carousel C's exit. We walked right up to the counter, gave our reservation number, and they had my rental contract in motion immediately. Everett grabbed the map the agent had drawn up for us with instructions to our hotel, along with the rental contract, and we walked down to exit 18 to catch the shuttle to our rental car.

We weren't on the shuttle long before he started acting silly. He was all in my face pretending to be a stranger, and I played his little silly game along with him.

"Excuse me Ms. I noticed how sexy you are and wanted to know if you were single?"

"No I'm not," I replied.

"Awe that's too bad because I sure would like to get to know you better. What are you doing here in Kansas City? Is this trip business or pleasure for you?"

"I'm meeting my boyfriend here for pleasure, and he might not appreciate you talking to me. But, then again, my husband might not appreciate me meeting him here for two days of ecstasy. I'm not interested in you anyway. Didn't I just see you macking on some sista you flew in with?.......... You must think you got game or something sucka, but know that you don't. And, I saw you."

He looked at me so funny, which made us both laugh like two bad kids.

"Welcome to Kansas City baby, I'm going to really make sure you enjoy yourself this weekend." He stated.

"Might I ask just how you plan to do that?"

"You'll see, I can't reveal all my secrets right up front. Plus you know my slogan, I can show you better than I can tell you."

"A-13 is the next stop," the shuttle driver yelled, which was the space that our rental car was parked in.

We gathered our luggage, exited the shuttle and loaded it into the car trunk. I got in the car, buckled up and pulled out the map to our hotel. Everett backed the car out of our spot and drove to the gate to be checked out.

"Where are you two headed," the gate attendant asked, while checking out our vehicle.

"The Grand Marquee Hotel in downtown Kansas City," we both replied at the same time.

"That's a beautiful hotel. You two will really enjoy yourselves there."

He looked at the driving route the clerk at the airport mapped out and insisted that we allow him to give us easier directions. As we pulled out of the parking lot, Everett thanked him for his assistance. He re-positioned the armrest, relaxed his arm and grabbed my hand. He tenderly kissed my fingers and cupped my hand for the remainder of our ride to the hotel.

We discussed how much we'd missed each other and the activities we wanted to do over the weekend. Finally, a street sign showing the remaining mileage before our exit came up. We could see the hotel towering above a few of the buildings downtown. However, when we pulled up in front of the hotel, it was then that it became obvious to us that we had definitely selected a beautiful hotel. The landscaping was indeed beautiful, and we both gazed at the building in amazement for a few seconds. The valet walked up to the car and asked if we wanted valet parking. Once we informed him that we would be using their services, we grabbed our bags, picked up the parking ticket and walked inside to the elevator.

Everett was still giving that bomb elevator romance, which made my eyes spin to the back of my head and started my juices flowing. When the elevator door opened, I felt like pushing the door button to ride one additional time. I could have gone for another round of affection, which I had truly been missing. Instead, we got off and headed for the front desk.

The clerk gave us our key to room 3032 and sent us on our way with instructions. As we approached the double doors, we could see that we had really gotten much more than we expected with that particular hotel.

"Oh my God, Everett, this hotel has a complete shopping mall, with restaurants galore. I didn't realize that any of this was located here when you told me this is where we would be staying."

"I picked this hotel strictly for the picture that was posted on the Internet. The agent mentioned that this hotel had a mall attached to it, but I didn't imagine it would be this big," he replied.

We made it to our room, and the first thing we noticed was the massive windowpane and the view of a huge pond that surrounded the back of the hotel. There was a beautiful covered deck and a bridge in the center of the pond which instantly captured our attention.

"Kyra, you know we have to find our way out to that covered deck. It's mandatory that I hold you out there under the moonlight tonight."

"That sounds great, but first, I want to give you something."

Everett sat at the foot of the bed and gave me his undivided attention. I reached into the gift bag I brought for him and pulled out the genie bottle, which had been nicely wrapped. He removed the bow, the wrapping, and the cork. Into his hand, he poured the scrolled message with a dark purple-coiled string and tarnished ring around it. As he unrolled the message, colorful glitter spilled all over the comforter and the area rug on the floor. I smiled as I looked on because there was glitter all over him, too. But what I admired most was that he didn't mind the mess one bit; he was more concerned with reading the message.

While he read out loud to me, I pulled each item out of his gift bag and laid them by his side. As he read the specific purpose of each item, he smiled, and when he made it to his Tazmanian Devil Photo Album, he had to stop reading and look at the pictures that had been taken of us together.

"Kyra, you know you are just too much. Sometimes you leave me speechless, and I promise I never know what to expect from you when we're together."

"Good, I like it that way. Sometimes I don't always know how you're going to respond to my thoughtfulness. I just do these things because I want you to have memories of us that outshine some of your other memories."

"You always surprise me. And it's the little things that you do that have me so gone for you."

"Oh! So you're gone for me?" I asked.

"Hell yeah! You know I am. If I wasn't, I wouldn't be spending over a thousand dollars to see you for less than 48 hours this weekend."

Deep within, I knew that I had gone all out for this man to make our last trip together memorable. I tried to be secretive about my actions to pull off my surprise, so I handed him the message to get him back on track while snapping my fingers at him. "Okay Everett, get back on track. There are still some real good trinkets left."

As he lifted the paper to read the rest of his message, he smiled.

"Thank you baby," he motioned with his mouth, as he sat the paper and the bottle on the bed.

"You're welcome, but I'm still not finished yet. I have two more gifts for you."

His eyes got extremely big, once I reached down in the oversized teddy bear gift bag and pulled out the Sean John jean outfit and sweater.

"Damn Kyra! This is nice as hell. Out of all the jean outfits I have, I don't own any Sean John."

"You like it?"

"Hell yeah! It's me. I'm feeling this for real."

"I'm glad because I damn near searched all over Oklahoma for your size. Every clothing store I went to was sold out, and when I finally found this outfit, it was the last one in your size."

"I like it baby; thank you so much. I don't know if I could ever come up with some of the ideas that you come up with, but I have loved them all."

"I'm glad, but I still have one more gift to go Everett. I tried to save the best for last"

He leaned back on the bed and looked at me with delight in his eyes. I reached into the bag one last time, and I pulled out a manila envelope, which contained a bound, paperback, copy of a book I was writing. It was full of pictures and had been dedicated to him.

"DAMN girl! You're writing a book, and the first copy of your book is dedicated to me. Wow baby, this is an honor; I don't even know what to say."

"Everett, before I started seeing you, I was really struggling with the completion of my book. My family problems, writer's block and no one to share my heartaches with prevented me from making my dream a reality. You gave me hope; you gave me a friend to confide in; you showed an interest in me when my own mate didn't, which inspired me to get back on task. You have motivated me in so many ways without even knowing it, which is why I'm giving you the first copy."

Out of all the gifts I had given him that evening, it was quite obvious to me that my book would be the one he cherished most. I sat on the foot of the bed next to him, and when he looked at me, I gracefully nodded my head and winked at him. I knew that I had been successful in accomplishing my mission from day one, which was to show him how special he was to me. Words could not describe the look on his face, but if I had to provide an example, I would say that he had a look of real confusion. He appeared to clearly be as puzzled and confused as I. "Affairs are never like this on T.V.," I thought to myself. But, this wasn't television, and the complexity of our situation was sure to increase after we spent the weekend making love.

"Come on Kyra, we need to get out of this room and find that deck," he suggested as he grabbed my hand. We walked into the mall and out of a back door to the deck. While exiting, I noticed extremely large snowflakes falling from the sky. They were so large I had to comment on them.

"Those snowflakes look like they're on steroids to me." I stated.

"You're silly. Do you still want to go to the deck, or do you just want to get something to eat?" He asked.

"Yeah, I'd rather eat. What about you?"

"You know I want to eat for sure. But, I'd rather go out on the deck first. This snow gives me another reason to be all over you. Besides, I'm a real man. I'm not afraid of the snow and ain't no snow flakes keeping me inside, so here take my coat."

"I'm not afraid of the snow either. I'm afraid of being cold." I quickly cut him off and replied.

"There's a coffee shop right by the door. We'll go back and get a cup of coffee and then go to the deck."

I didn't particularly like coffee, but I knew I'd better get something hot, if I wanted to stay warm. I asked Everett if he had ever had cappuccino. He hadn't, so I encouraged him to try a cup. I ordered two regular cups of French Vanilla, and they whipped us up a fresh blend while Everett stood behind me hugging my waist. When they were ready, he grabbed them both off the counter and handed me my drink. He wrapped it in a napkin to make sure I didn't burn myself, and then covered it with a lid. We exited the coffee shop hand-in-hand and walked the snow covered trail to the deck.

"Kyra, this is really nice baby. Thanks for meeting me because I really wanted to see you."

"Same here. Everett, I couldn't think of any other person, besides Taylor, who I'd rather be standing here with. Thank you so much for making this happen for me this weekend."

We stood out on the deck holding each other, talking and sipping cappuccino. Neither the cool temperature nor the snow really seemed to bother us one bit. The moon and stars were positioned perfectly in the sky. The snow fell on the water just right, and holding Everett felt great. The water sprinkling from the fountains in the center of the pond made the most beautiful designs, as it hit the water. The vibration from each drop made rings in the water, while the moon glistened on the pond. The only other romantic gesture that could have made this moment more picture perfect would have been for him to get down on one knee and serenade me.

The moment was so captivating. It actually amazed me as I stood there thinking of how so many of our special moments had been like a book of stories. As I gazed out into the night daydreaming, I focused on one particular snowflake as it was falling from the sky. It was so beautiful. I could only admire its beauty, as it gracefully floated from the sky into the pond and dissolved on contact. The very thing that I had just observed with that snowflake was a perfect metaphor of what was happening between us. When we initially started talking in August of 2001, I floated on air from the time I saw him in Woody's to the arrival of his very first visit. My visit to Detroit and my departure in December is when our beautiful relationship hit the water, and Kimberlin's moving in is when our special bond dissolved.

The conversation we shared on the deck was stimulating and mentally rewarding, but it was getting colder and my hands were freezing. The tip of my nose had become red, and I was sniffling. I could have stayed out there securely wrapped in Everett's arms for another hour with the way our evening was going. But he could see that I was cold and insisted that we go inside to thaw out.

"Kyra Murrell, it's getting a little chilly baby, and your nose is red and ice cold," he stated as he led me off the deck.

"Yeah, it is a little chilly."

"I better get you out of this cold, before you get sick."

"Yeah Papa, you better, or I might not be able to fulfill your fantasy tonight."

"Kyra as bad as I want you, you could be sick, have one good eye, be frost bit, whatever. I wouldn't give a damn. As long as I have waited on you, we're making love tonight."

He stopped walking in mid-stride, eased up on me with puckered lips, kissed my nose and stated,

"Oh yeah, you're fulfilling fantasies tonight baby. As soon as I get into my romantic mindset, we're making love. Knees will be touching elbows in 3032 tonight. You can forget that hot shower and holding me shit for the evening. It's a new format for tonight."

"There's a new format tonight. And what is the new format, if I might ask?" He looked over at me with this devious look in his eyes and replied.

"First of all I'm taking charge, and the format goes like this: We're taking a hot shower, then it's gon be some caressing, talking-moaning, grinding, screaming, holding, and if necessary we'll repeat that cycle in that order, excluding the hot shower. You're gonna be satisfied with the kind of skills I'm bringin to K.C. all the way for the D."

"Shoot, we need to be going to the room right now then because I'm long overdue," I replied.

We laughed and walked back inside the mall. We walked down to a bar and grill restaurant located in the food court and ordered some appetizers and drinks. We sat near an enclosed deck, which overlooked the pond, so we could admire the scenery. Everett just kept looking over at me. It was as if he was searching for words to convince me that we were meant to be. Finally, he grabbed my hands and tenderly stroked them with his thumbs and then his lips. I watched his mouth, as he licked his lips to moisten them, then applied some additional chap stick to keep them moist. A kiss would have set the moment, but somehow the server brought out our food, and my cell phone rang at the same time, which disturbed the mood.

Bruce decided to call and see if I had made it safely, which shocked the heck out of me. I was so caught up in what I was doing with Everett that calling to check in totally slipped my mind. I was really surprised that he was concerned enough to call and check on me. I was so speechless that I really didn't know what to say. I told him I would call home later to give him my room number and speak to the baby. Everett looked concerned when he learned that it was

Bruce. But when I hung up the phone, I explained to him that he was just calling to check in.

While we discussed what we had been missing in each other, we satisfied our appetites on Buffalo wings, potato skins, beer and mudslides. One issue Everett discussed with me during our meal was that he was initially trying to honor my attempt to end our relationship. However, when I shared with him that I had seen Calvin a time or two since the detailing shop, it bothered him. He was jealous of Calvin, which caused me to laugh at him.

"Calvin made a brother say forget space. I know how men are, and he was trying to become your other man on the sly."

"Boy you're crazy; Calvin and I aren't thinking about each other. We've seen each other out twice since the detailing shop, and I don't want him."

"That's why I'm concerned. How you go from not seeing that man at all to casually bumping into him all of a sudden. He makes sure he's where he thinks you're going to be, and you don't even see that it's a set up."

"Well what do you think I'm going to do with him? Hell, I'm a married woman."

He looked at me with his eyes bucked wide open, and replied,

"Don't go there. Look at us, MARRIED WOMAN!" We laughed, and then he stated, "I think we better leave on that note before I get myself into trouble." He drank the last of his beer, paid the tab, and we left the bar.

Everett wanted to get another cup of cappuccino before going to the room. He claimed that I had gotten him hooked.

"Aren't you full? If not, you should be."

"I am full, but I'm addicted. Wait until I tell all my friends that my uppity girlfriend has me liking an unmanly drink like cappuccino."

"You better clarify which girlfriend you're talking about because from what Kat described, Kimberlin doesn't seem classy enough to even desire the corner store cappuccino." I sarcastically stated.

Everett was visibly irritated with my comment. I could tell that he thought I was trying to be nasty, so he ignored me. We came upon a wishing fountain, which stretched at least half a mile, located by the food court. Everett pulled two coins out of his pocket and handed one to me. I looked over the second level balcony at the water streaming down below in the fountain and really thought about what I might wish for. I wanted to make sure that I used my wish wisely.

Everett quickly pitched his coin into the water, in a matter of seconds, appearing to give his wish little to no thought at all. There I stood still thinking, "Awe, what might I wish for?" Then finally it came to me. As he impatiently stared at me, I closed my eyes, held the coin up in my right hand and made a silent wish. I rolled my dime to the tip of my fingers and threw it into the water.

"With as long as it took you to make that wish, Kyra, I sure hope it comes true."

"What did you wish for Everett?" I asked.

"I'm not telling you now, but if it comes true, I'll tell you later."

"What if I don't want to wait until later?"

"Then you're going to be in bad shape because I'm not telling you and take a chance on messing up my wish."

While walking away from the fountain, I turned up my nose at him and stated, "So! I really didn't want to know what you wished for anyway."

16

The Room

Eleven fifty-two flashed on the clock, as we entered the room. I walked in behind Everett, so I pushed the door closed and locked it. I sat on the edge of the chair near the door, while he unpacked his bag. He pulled out some shower gel, then motioned for me to come take a shower with him. He stripped down to his boxers and strutted from one side of the room to the other like he had real sex appeal. I smiled while thinking to myself; "Look at his prissy ass pulling out scented shower gel and body lotion. He has some nerve calling me uppity."

"Kyra, I'm about to jump in the shower, are you going to join me?"

"I'll be in there in one minute."

He strolled on into the bathroom singing; "Love You Down," by Silk. I recognized that he was extremely anxious about making love to me, so he sang love songs to set the mood. Everett had waited so long for this moment. I'm sure he probably felt like a star athlete, right before the big game, on Super Bowl Sunday. But, because he kept rushing me to come get in the shower, I was about to help him experience what double overtime before the big score felt like.

I decided to take my time about going into the bathroom. I had acquired cold feet and was in no rush to make love. The guarded side of me had to make sure that being sexually intimate with him was something I really wanted for myself, so I pranced around the room doing a bunch of superficial time wasters. When I got in the shower, Everett was somewhat irritated and asked in an agitated tone,

"What took you so long?"

"I had a few things I wanted to do before I got in the tub."

"Oh! So just make me wait? Well I'm about to get out now."

"I'm sorry, I didn't think you would mind. But don't act like you haven't waited on me before."

"Yeah I've waited too long, and I'm tired of waiting, chump." He replied, while pulling me towards him for a kiss. And that's when all conversation abruptly ended.

Everett attached himself to me so tight, I thought for a minute that we were Siamese Twins. He wouldn't back up off of me for anything. He wanted to be close to me and stayed on my phat rump like a guided missile on a locked target. As always, after a few feels, he was ready to get out of the shower and play. He grabbed his towel then put up two fingers. "I know that wasn't your way of telling me to get out in two minutes. Was it?" I asked, while he was stepping out of the tub. I was infamous for long showers and he wanted to make sure that I wasn't about to keep him waiting all night.

While waiting on me, he rubbed lotion on his body, lit candles and played soft music to enhance the mood that was already brewing. He poured himself a drink, laid out some dainty lingerie he purchased for me in Detroit and fluffed his pillows. "Kyra I'm waiting on you." He yelled, while propping himself up against the headboard to read chapter one of the book I had given him.

"I'll be out shortly." I yelled back to him, as I lathered my body an additional time unnecessarily.

"Okay, just take your time because you're going to do that anyway," he replied.

Once I got out of the shower, I dried off, put on my lucky T-shirt, sprayed on a tease of perfume in the right places and rubbed lotion on my body. I walked into the room to get my toothbrush and stopped for a second to admire Everett, as he sat quietly reading to himself. He was so engaged in my darn book that I had to act as though I was clearing my throat just to get his attention. He briefly pulled the book away from his face, long enough to say a couple of words to me.

"Hey, sexy, you need to be over here in my arms."

"I sure do and if you give me a few minutes to brush my teeth, I'll be right with you."

"Hold on, I got something special I want you to wear for me tonight." He reached over on the pillow next to him and grabbed the lingerie he bought.

"Wear this for me tonight please," he stated while extending his arm and handing me the nighty.

"Oh, what, my T-shirt isn't sexy enough for you?"

"Yeah babe. I really love your T-Shirt. It's just not special enough for this occasion. I wanted you to wear something sexy and sleek for me tonight. I got this outfit from Victoria's Secret because I wanted to be sure that what you wore was perfect for tonight."

I took the lingerie into the bathroom with me, and he went right back to reading. I slipped into the nighty, brushed my teeth then returned to the bedroom. After I saw myself, I could understand why he was so fond of that particular nighty. I was looking really delicious in it, and I felt tremendously sexy. Once he laid eyes on me, he was ready to venture inside the domains of my fantasy island. And I was ready to expose him to a warm, moist tropical place only I knew about. He sat his book on the nightstand and gawked at me for a second, then spoke.

"Come here baby and let me hold you." He softly stated.

"It's about time, you started paying me some attention," I replied.

"I can't help it that your book is so interesting. You should be glad it was hard for me to put it down."

"I'm really glad that you enjoyed it. But, right now I want to be close to you. I need you to hold me." I replied in the most innocent tone, while grabbing his arms and draping them around me.

Everett gently moved my arms and slid out of bed with his towel loosely wrapped around his waist. I looked at him and while rolling my eyes, I asked; "Now where are you going? We have played this hold out game long enough." I couldn't take it any longer because I was ready to make love to this man. "I'm about to fix me a drink, get the mood just right, and then I'm gon turn you out." He replied in the sexiest tone.

As he moved about the room, I impatiently watched him. He poured himself another drink, and then leaned down to blow out four of the five candles burning.

While he was getting back into bed, I turned up the music that was softly playing and fluffed my pillows. I knew the moment that we'd been waiting for had finally arrived. I wasn't quite comfortable on my pillows and had to adjust them one additional time. I had this obsession about making love on flat pillows. And as long as we had waited for our moment of passion, there was no way bold pillow positioning was going to be the excuse for me getting a poor performance rating.

Once Everett slid back into bed, I must have missed something somewhere between him turning off the lamp and walking to the bed. When he got under the covers that brother was butt booty naked, and I never even saw him remove his towel. He touched me a little slow at first, but the more secure he felt about making love to me, the busier his hands became. Of course, he did his busy hands safe test first. When he passed the rubbing, feeling, touching stage without being scolded, or having his face cupped, he knew he was about to enter the Zone.

But, just entering the zone wasn't going to be good enough for him. He was in search of the big score, so he rolled over on top of me and passionately kissed me. My nipples immediately became erect because I was hot, soaking wet and ready to gyrate my goldmine. My nipples bulged through my top, which was a real turn on for him. I tightly gripped his butt, pulling him closer to me, and

137

sure enough that appeared to be just the invitation he actually needed to proceed to the next level.

He remained very patient with me, as he went from one sexual phase to the next. His behavior was highly cautious. It was as though he was testing me to see if I was going to back out or stop him just when things got heated. However, as good as I was feeling at that moment, the last thing I was thinking about was stopping him. I wanted him in my personal space, and there was just no turning back at that point. During my pillow talk, it was my plan to let him know that I wasn't holding back anything, and I wanted to feel him deep inside of me, once we got down to handling our business.

Things were a little slow at first, but I must admit that the way Everett caressed my body was like magic. He sucked my breast like a brand new breast pump and surveyed every inch of my body like an explorer. His foreplay was so bomb that it could have been featured on the Discovery Channel. Shit, and the technique he used to slide my panties off was so unique that I didn't even realize they had been removed until I felt the heat from his breath hovering over my pubic hairs. From that point on, I was under his spell. As he went from one spot on my body to the next, he tenderly rubbed my belly with his face. I could feel his whiskers and hear each breath he took, as he rested his head inches below my navel. He kept his head there for a moment and just held me. The warmth of our bodies together, skin to skin was marvelous and a major turn on for me.

"Where would he go from there," I wondered. I could tell that he was contemplating his next move as well. "Should he taste my fruit snacks or shouldn't he?" I'm sure he thought to himself a time or two and as horny as I was, it was a good thing he didn't ask me for my opinion. There would have been no words for my reply, only two hands pushing his head in a downward direction towards my sweet lickables.

He lifted his face off of my stomach and kissed my inner thighs. My mind was in disbelief. I just kept repeating to myself, "Damn I can't believe this is happening." He paused briefly, as I grabbed a pillow and buried my face in it to scream. That small distraction would only be a brief one and within seconds he bit my ass cheeks to get me focused on what was about to happen. I jumped a little because it tickled and once I relaxed again, his face went right back into my spot, tongue first. I was no longer in control, my legs fell open without resistance, and like a swarm of hungry bees all over a honeycomb; he was snacking on my sweetness.

For a brief second, I considered calling it quits. Then, I thought about my behavior, versus the climax I was about to experience and saw no reason to turn back. We had already crossed the line, plus Everett had an erection so unreal to my eyes, I knew I had to feel what he was working with. It would have been so foolish for me to waste the moment, so I laid back, relaxed and allowed him to take me there. Everett, rose to his knees, slid on his condom, and gently entered my world. He made love to me like he had just received his Bachelor's, Master's and PhD in Sexual Stimulation and Positions, with honors.

After round four, I laid next to him thinking about the way he worked his joystick. I was hooked, better yet whipped from the experience of having one orgasm after another. I felt like calling him, "King," because Mr. Barnett had not just made love to me, but that brotha slung enough beef to make my legs go mush repeatedly that night. His skills earned him the title of "Multiple Orgasm King" in my life. I mean, after the work he put in, it would have been very appropriate for him to walk around the room with his chest stuck out. No one had ever made love to me like that before. After that, Everett had my body tingling, my legs shaking, my juices flowing and my mind was really gone.

"That was good," he stated while breathing heavily. But, I already knew that, so there was no need for me to respond to his comment at all. It did feel good to hear him compliment me on my ability to please him sexually because I was out of practice.

I had almost forgotten what it was like to have someone make great love to me. But, Everett Barnett refreshed my memory and I was A-dick-ded.

17

Again

I glanced over at the clock, and it was already three-thirty in the morning. I had become extremely sleepy and felt like thirty minutes of rest would do me well. It had been a very long day for me, which is why my eyes were probably burning. My sexual encounter had exhausted my last bit of energy, and I was determined to get some sleep before the Saturday morning sunrise.

We had plans to get out early that morning and do some site seeing. But, I knew I wouldn't make it if I stayed up any longer.

"I'm going to rest my eyes for a little while, Everett." I said, while kissing his lips and snuggling up in his arms.

"Ok baby, get some rest. I'm not sleepy. I'm going to read a little more of this book."

He turned the lamp back on next to the bed and sipped down the rest of his drink. He propped up his pillows, cradled me in his arms and quietly read. He initially positioned his body so that he could comfortably hold me and read at the same time. Once I dozed off, he interrupted my sleep with his loud laughing. I looked over at him a few times with squinted eyes and knew that I needed to move out of his arm if I wanted to really get some good rest. Shortly after I moved, Everett let out another loud chuckle. "Everett! What are you laughing about?" I asked. He told me I was silly and that he was really enjoying my book. I couldn't believe that he was still up reading and was one page short of chapter four. He didn't want to put the book down and go to bed because he was too anxious to find out the outcome.

Finally he suggested that I wake up and read the last chapter with him. "I wrote it. I already know what it's about." I stated. He smacked his lips and jokingly replied, "Well go on to sleep then, Party Pooper." I felt a little recharged after my power nap, so I comfortably positioned myself in his arms, and we read the last few pages together.

The purple candle Everett lit was still burning. The flicker from the flame captured my attention, as I went into a blank stare. I thought about my initial purpose for purchasing that particular candle. We had surely lived up to its purpose. Every king should indeed make love to the flickering flame of a royal colored candle, while every queen reaps the benefits.

My imagination got the best of me, as I replayed our initial moment of passion over in my mind. My thoughts put me in the mood once again. I was still in need of some romance, so I rubbed Everett's chest for a while and my hands slowly started to wander. I rubbed his stomach, caressed his thighs, and slowly moved on to his PPP's (private personal parts). Once he became erect again, my juices started to naturally flow. His partner in crime was standing at attention, like a boot camp solider and it was so obvious that he, too, was ready for round five.

"Forget waiting," I thought, as I straddled him and asked, "Are you sleepy?"
"No! I'm ready for another round of one on one with Mrs. Murrell," he quickly replied.

Another round was exactly what I had in mind, so he tossed his book on the nightstand and grabbed a condom. I turned the faint music playing in the background back up, while he turned off the lamp. Round five, six and seven of Barnett vs. Murrell was even more passionate than round one through four. I was feeling good while he penetrated me. Hell, for a minute I thought that I had lost my vision, due to my eyes rolling so far up in my head. After we finished, had I been a sista who smoked, I would have crawled out of bed to have myself a Queen B victory puff. But, since I wasn't, I eased my backside closer to Everett and slept like a newborn baby.

Saturday morning, the sun was beaming through the window right in my face. It appeared as though the day had come much faster than Everett had the night before. The light interrupted my sleep, so I fumbled under the covers for my nightclothes. I found my panties at the foot of the bed and my top was on the floor. "Wow! I don't remember my top flying across the room," I thought. We must have been very anxious to get busy.

I snatched my top off the floor, as I walked to the bathroom. I washed my face then made sure I brushed my teeth thoroughly before saying anything to Everett that morning. I was not one for talking to anyone with morning breath. And just because he had given it to me like a stud, it wasn't bomb enough to make me violate that rule.

While looking at myself in the bathroom mirror, I had suddenly become shy for some reason, and my conscience was trying to kill my moment of pleasure. "Too late to be shy now. You weren't acting shy last night." Why and where the guilt was coming from had me completely confused. I had just experienced one of the best evenings of my life in a very long time, and I was feeling too good to entertain my cock blocking conscience. I channeled my thoughts on something else because I was determined that I was not going to second guess my behavior and returned back to the room.

18

Where Do We Go From Here

Everett and I always had great discussions. The conversation we had that particular morning seemed to be one of our best. The minutes turned into hours and we were about to let the day completely get away from us as usual.

"Are you hungry?" I asked.

"Yes, I am, but I could think of a number of things I would rather eat that don't require us leaving the room at all," he replied.

"Ok, get your mind out of the gutter," I stated while hitting him in his stomach and easing out of bed.

I suggested that we get up and get out before it got late. I jumped in the shower, while Everett ironed his clothes. Once I finished showering, I came out of the bathroom draped in a towel. I was brushing my teeth, but wanted to ask him a question at the same time. As I was presenting my question, a drip of toothpaste ran down my bottom lip. Everett walked up on me feeling super affectionate and licked the dripping toothpaste off my chin.

"Yucky! Yuck! Yuck!" I said, before I totally realized what he had done.

"Girl, if you let me, I'd drink your bath water."

"Damn Everett! After that crap you just pulled, I bet you would, too." I was in total shock. I shook my head at him, turned and walked back towards the bathroom. "This man has completely lost his mind." I mumbled. But, his actions did make me think I was tremendously special to him because though I am Taylor's mom, I'm not licking toothpaste off of her face for any reason.

When we were dressed, we tried to leave the hotel to see the sites of the city. As we were exiting, Everett had to stop and get a cup of cappuccino. He had truly become addicted and wasn't leaving without getting a cup. The night before it was French Vanilla, so he wanted to try a different flavor. He ordered Hazelnut, but discovered that French Vanilla was his favorite because he claimed it reminded him of something.

"I like French Vanilla best because it reminds me of someone I tasted last night," he stated.

"I think you're hooked period Everett. It has nothing to do with the flavor."

"You're wrong, Boo. It has absolutely everything to do with the flavor."

"Oh, so we could market my erotic body juices and people would buy them?"

"We could market your juices and brothas and sista's would most certainly buy them. Kyra, your taste is so good that you'd stay sold out."

"Well I'm going to leave that alone because I certainly don't want to think of any sista's tasting me." I replied while laughing.

The Concierge greeted us with the biggest smile, and then contacted the valet attendant to have our car pulled around. Everett opened my door to assist me with getting in, gently shut it, and then walked around the front of the car making faces at me. He was so silly and so much fun to be around. I think what I enjoyed most was how he always found ways to make me smile.

Actually, Everett was everything Bruce once was and spending time with him helped clarify for me the wonderful relationship Bruce and I had truly lost. Many of his behaviors reminded me of the romance I once shared with Bruce. The more I thought about my relationship with Everett, the more I realized that what we shared could never be anything more than just a romantic get away. I could finally see that it would not benefit either of us in any manner to elevate our relationship to the next level. After being involved in an extra martial affair with him, I was sure that I would not be able to trust him and vise versa; for that reason alone, we would always be nothing more than weekend lovers.

Kansas City's famous Bar B. Q. joint was packed when we arrived. To waste a little time, we stood out in the parking lot taking pictures and throwing snowballs. I bent down to scoop up another heap of snow and my cell phone rang. It was Bruce calling to see how my trip was going. As I moved away from Everett to talk to Bruce, his phone rang also, and it was Kimberlin. I spread my arms opened and shrugged my shoulders, whispering, "What is this, a set up?" We pointed at each other, smiling, while continuing to put distance between us in order to talk in private.

"What's going on with you Kyra?" Bruce asked.
"Not too much. I'm about to get something to eat. How's the baby?"
"She's fine. She misses you and I do, too."
"Well, kiss her for me."
"I will. You have fun Kyra, and I'll call you later."

I had the eeriest feeling after Bruce hung up. Guilt shredded me to pieces like ground meat, and I felt sorry for him for the first time in years. Everett discontinued his call shortly after I did and had the nerve to joke about the possibility of Bruce and Kimberlin being together when they called. The sad part about this entire situation was that neither one of us seemed to really care about what was going on back at home with our mates, until they called, and neither of us said much about our conversations, out of fear of disturbing the evening. We went on with our activities without ever mentioning our mates again, but it was clear that my conversation with Bruce certainly changed my mood.

Everett had never eaten Bar B. Q. in Kansas before, but he was truly a Bar B. Q. lover. I watched him as he took the first bite of his food, and I couldn't resist asking him if he liked it. He nodded "yes," while grabbing a napkin to wipe sauce off of his cheek.

"See Everett, you've tried two different things this weekend that you thought were great," I stated.

"No! I tried three things this weekend I thought were great," he replied. I knew the third was my good loving, but there was no need to boast about my abilities. Though his comment was an ego booster for me, it was one of those comments that didn't require a response.

We finished our meal and sat around engaged in small talk, which ultimately blossomed into this profound discussion about extra marital affairs. Both of us concluded that there was a lot at risk if we were ever exposed. Our discussion put a lot of issues on the table for the other to think about. As we exited the restaurant, it was visible in the expression on both of our faces that we were thinking about comments made and considering where we would go from that point. Everett didn't say much on the way back to the hotel. He just held my hand and occasionally looked over at me with the saddest eyes.

We were both quiet once we made it back to the room. I believe we knew and clearly understood that our romance was about to seriously end. We couldn't go on at the rate we were going for the rest of our lives because there was just no way that it could realistically work. I also knew that no matter how perfect we appeared to be for each other, we were involved in relationships outside of the one we shared.

I considered Kimberlin, as well and knew that she deserved something better and was a victim of circumstance. Guilt briefly overwhelmed me once again about my ability to dog out another woman.

Yeah, I had knowingly dogged her by continuing to see Everett and that bothered me. I sat at the foot of the bed, completely disgusted with myself and watched the news. I grabbed a blanket to cover myself because I had a slight chill and draped it over my lower body. Everett sat over in the corner of the room, in a chair, watching me for as long as he could.

"Kyra, come over here and let me hold you." I looked over at him, but didn't move.

"Hold me." I repeated in a confused tone.

"Yes! Let me hold you. I want to hold you for a while, if you don't mind?"

"Why would I mind?"

"Because you haven't said much since we left the restaurant. There's nothing you can say that will ever change the way I feel about you, so don't shut down on me."

As empty and as guilty as I was feeling inside, I needed to be held. I grabbed my blanket, walked over to him and sat on his lap, draping the blanket across us both. I laid my head on his shoulder, and he turned and kissed my forehead. He cradled me in his arms, which seemed to immediately sooth the emptiness and guilt I felt. The longer he cradled me, the more relaxed I became. Finally, I closed my eyes and fell asleep.

I woke up hours later only to discover that Everett had laid me in the bed. I looked around for him, but he wasn't in the room. I could hear water running in the bathroom and assumed that he was taking a shower. I crawled out of bed, undressed and walked into the bathroom to join him. I slightly pulled back the curtains and noticed him wiping water from his face with his bare hands. I entered the shower from the back, eased up on him and gently hugged him from behind.

"Hey handsome, how come you didn't wake me up?" I asked.

"You looked like such an angel and were resting so peacefully, I just didn't want to disturb you."

"So you were going to just allow me to sleep our entire last evening together away?"

"Yep! I am not in agreement with discontinuing our relationship. As far as I'm concerned this is not our last evening together. One of the greatest experiences in life that ever happened for me was reuniting with you. You are my friend; I love the activities we do together, and the time we share is priceless. I'm not letting someone who makes me feel so good walk out of my life just like that. So do what you feel you need to do, but I'm not going anywhere,"

What could I say that might change his mind? Actually, I needed to ask myself, "If I really even wanted to change his mind?" I didn't know what I wanted for myself, so how was I going to even try to put my feelings for him into words? I stood there speechless with water pounding on my shoulders, while I held him. "Let's get out of the shower together for once," he suggested. I grabbed a towel, placed it on the floor, and we both stepped out of the tub, one behind the other. He draped a towel around his waist and handed one to me.

We couldn't see anything, due to the steam, so he grabbed a hand towel off the rack, wiped off the mirror and eased up behind me stating, "Look at this beautiful woman I'm holding in my arms. Now look at this beautiful couple. How could you want to end chemistry like this, Kyra?" His question caught me off guard. Again, I had no reply for him. He turned off the bathroom light and carried me into the bedroom. He gently laid me on the bed and began kissing me. His passion would lead to hours of lovemaking, moans and ecstasy that would take us into Sunday morning.

I quickly sprung up about eleven-thirty that morning thinking we had slept through checkout. I shook Everett for a while, but he didn't want to wake up. "Everett it's almost checkout time." He mumbled something, as I was walking into the bathroom to get a glass of water to pour on him. But he must have sensed that I was up to something because just as I turned to walk out with my cup of water, he was at the door waiting.

"And just what do you think you're about to do with that water?" He asked smiling.
"Put it in the iron." I sassily replied.

19

Never Can Say Goodbye

We checked out slightly after noon, had lunch, and then returned our rental car. We arrived at the airport three hours early, thinking that the lines would be extremely long. What we discovered once we arrived was that travelers weren't traveling like we expected and lines at the ticket counters were quite short. We hoped that earlier flights would be somewhat empty too. I attempted to change our initial flight reservations, but there were only seats available on the flight to Oklahoma. I didn't want to leave Everett sitting in the airport alone, so I kept my original departure time.

The clerk pointed us in the direction of the terminal, and Everett grabbed my hand. Once we arrived at our location, it was so amazing to us both that our departure gates were side by side. We found seats centrally located between both service counters and sat our bags down. Everett immediately noticed a coffee shop right across from us and had to get a cup of cappuccino.

"Boy you are hooked."
"Yeah I'm hooked, but at least I can count on it being a part of my life for as long as I want it to be."

I could see he was trying to irritate me. So I decided not to even go there with him. He stood in line and looked over at me, like he was extremely frustrated with the way our weekend was ending. Once he ordered his French Vanilla Cappuccino, a female attendant at the counter started flirting with him. He was over at that coffee shop, smiling from ear-to-ear, until I walked up on him and kissed the back of his neck.

"Is that your wife?" the attendant asked.

"No, I'm standing here, just because," I arrogantly replied.
He burst out laughing, and then stated, "Yes, this is my wife, she's just trippin."

She gave me the craziest look and must have felt driven to say something. I could tell she felt embarrassed because she complimented us on being a very attractive couple, and then her attitude immediately changed. I thanked her for noticing, with a somber expression on my face, and moved away from the counter pulling Everett along.

Once we were far enough away from people, I told Everett to be more respectful in the future and that would prevent me from showing my butt on him in public.

"Stop trippin and give me your hand. You are so uppity sometimes," he quickly replied.
"I'm not trippin, I'm serious."
"Well, you can't be serious because you said that we were done after today."
"I know what I said, but I still don't want to see you flirting with anyone else."
"Come on! I respect you too much for that Kyra."
"Well I guess I couldn't tell, since all I could see was all thirty-two of your damn teeth."
"Ok. I'm done with this conversation. You want to argue, and I'm not about to go there with you. Like I said you need to stop trippin."

As we sat by our gate, Everett held my hand, tenderly caressing my fingers. He looked at his watch a few times, as if he was wishing time would just stand still.

"Everett, what are you thinking about?"
"I'm thinking how special you are to me, whether I did the right thing by allowing Kimberlin to move to Detroit and most of all, how much I wish the two of us could be together on a full time basis."

151

"I wish we could be together, as well. But realistically you and I both know that if we were dating on a full time basis our relationship wouldn't be this great."

"I think it would be even better Kyra. I have developed a love for you that feels really good. You and I have done things people only dream about in a lifetime. We have lived a fantasy that I will take to my grave, and I hope that these memories are memories that you'll cherish a lifetime also."

"Everett, you know that we have shared some wonderful memories, and I will never forget those times either."

"So does this mean that you are going to continue to see me once you get back to Oklahoma?"

"I can't really say. You know me I'm on one day, off the next. It truly depends on what I really want for myself, once I get settled in at home."

Everett was clearly displeased with where our conversation was going. Suddenly he went into a blank stare and became extremely quiet. I wanted to ask him what he truly expected out of the relationship, but instead I decided to allow him to have his moment to meditate, so I quietly sat watching people as they passed me in the terminal.

Families traveling together often caught my attention. Each group who walked by appeared to be so peaceful and happy. The happiness I observed on the faces of children traveling with both parents almost broke me. I thought about my very own daughter and the possibility of her never experiencing an enjoyable vacation with both of her parents. That thought alone truly broke my heart because I realized that if Bruce and I didn't resolve our issues soon, poor Taylor might never have the opportunity to experience a family vacation.

The thought of Taylor and my desire for her to be raised in a home with both of her parents consumed my mind. Before I knew it, I was questioning my actions and had actually started to regret my decision to have an affair all together.

"What the hell are you doing here, Kyra," I kept thinking to myself, as I looked over at Everett, who was still quiet. "This is a place you should be with your daughter and your husband," my conscience kept telling me. But how in the world was I supposed to make my relationship right between Bruce and I, when our problems had gotten so bad. Making something like a simple family outing actually happen for us was nothing more than a fictitious dream for me. While I was processing ways I could fix my marriage, Everett slowly stood up stating that he would be back.

As he walked away, he reached into his wallet and pulled out his calling card. He walked about fifty feet from where we were sitting over to a phone booth. I knew he was calling Kimberlin to check in. I thought his actions might have been motivated by our conversation. He hadn't called her all weekend, and I tried to understand why he felt motivated to call her all of a sudden. I figured guilt was probably eating him up as well. If not guilt, he was possibly trying to irritate me or make me jealous, which he had successfully accomplished. I already had to deal with the fact that he was going home to her waiting arms, but he certainly didn't have to throw it in my face. But, since he decided to put it out there like that, I was going to accept it like a woman.

I watched him as he talked on the phone. I don't think he ever really considered why I wanted to end our relationship. He only thought of his own personal needs and wants, which made him seem very selfish at times. What he was most concerned about was what he preferred. He didn't want to hear anything else; therefore, he totally blocked out all room for reasoning. I glanced over at him again and closely observed him, as he conversed with Kimberlin. His body language expressed the real pleasure he found in the woman who had become his new live in mate, and it drove me crazy. I wanted someone to love me just like that. I wanted someone to adore me just like that; I wanted someone to desire me and only me just…….. like…….. that.

When we were together, he always tried to hide what he truly felt for her. He always seemed to try to downplay what they shared, but actions don't lie. The way he smiled while talking with her was a statement in itself. I must admit that my final impression of their relationship did not settle well with me at all. However, taking the time to watch him talk to her was the best thing that happened for us that day. Seeing that kind of happiness on his face confirmed for me that I was in fact nothing more than that weekend get away for him, a get away I believe he honestly enjoyed when we were together. But when he returned home, he returned home to the person he considered his real woman. We had been living a major lie, a lie in which only time and space could adequately repair.

Observing him helped me understand that what I was lacking in my relationship with Bruce could not be lived on a part time basis through him. Once I returned home, Everett and I would have to put space between us. We were going to have to focus on the purpose of having the mates we had in our lives and move on. I was finally starting to see and accept what was destined to be for us. As he walked back, I stopped to lust one last time at his distinguished walk. "What a cutie," I thought to myself.

"Hey beautiful have you thought about what I said before I left to use the phone?"

"Yes, Everett, I sure did. I decided that you and I have something wonderful called friendship. It's a great friendship too and it should not be compromised for something that we both know is guaranteed to be short term or nothing more than a two day adventure. I love the way you have made me feel these past few months, and I will probably regret my decision to walk away from what we share. But, it is only right that I take into consideration what is best for both of our lives and not just mine. I have been selfish and self concerned since we've been dating. It's not right for me to infringe on your new relationship just because mine is a mess right now."

"Kyra, you can only do what I allow you to do. I meet up with you in these different states because I enjoy what we have. Why are you so concerned with Kimberlin? Let me worry about her. If I'm not concerned, then you shouldn't be."

"Everett, I have fallen in love with you. I don't want to wake up one morning hurting as bad as I do today because I'm torn between two men. Bruce has hurt me enough, and I don't want to go through this kind of pain again over a man who initially belonged to someone else. I knew I was wrong when I continued to pursue you after you told me about Kimberlin. Now feelings are involved, and because mine are so fragile right now, I've got to protect them. You can't guarantee me that you won't call me one day with news of marriage or a baby. I can't take that kind of pain. So, I'm going to remove myself from the situation before that happens."

"This is not what I want for us, Kyra, but I respect your decision and I'm going to try to honor your request. But I will never just walk out of your life."

No matter what Everett said, I wasn't willing to compromise my dignity any more than I already had for some part-time companionship. Terminating our affair was the best decision for us both, but for some reason I felt terrible. My legs felt mushy; my eyes started to burn, and my heart felt like five hundred pounds of weights had been placed on my chest. I knew when it finally came down to this decision for us, it would be hard to part. But Wow! My heart was breaking, and we still had at least thirty minutes to go before I had to board my plane.

Those thirty minutes were the longest thirty minutes of my life. They felt more like thirty years, as we sat watching the clock together. We didn't address our relationship anymore that evening. We both sat quietly and waited for the attendant to call for boarding. Right before boarding my plane, I remember looking into Everett's sad eyes one last time.

"Well Ky, that's your call."

"Yeah, I know. I had such a nice time with you this weekend. Thank you so much for everything and please make sure you call me and let me know you made it to Detroit safely." I sadly replied.

Everett kind of slowly nodded his head and then affectionately hugged me. He held me for a moment and softly kissed my forehead one last time. "I love you Kyra. Have a safe flight and I'll call you when I touch down." I grabbed my bag and walked to the back of the line.

Everett stood close by with his right hand in his pocket. He looked over at me, smiled a few times, softly kissed his left hand and blew me a tender kiss. At that point, my emotions would give me away. Tears fell from my eyes just as I made it to the ticket agent. After checking my identification, I was cleared to board my plane. I slowly turned and waved bye, then quietly motioned the words, "I love you, too."

I boarded my plane, put my luggage in the overhead bin and strapped myself into my seat. "Why didn't I just kiss the man goodbye one last time?" I kept repeating to myself, while looking out the window over at his plane. I wondered if it was foolish for me to call his cell phone to request that he give me a kiss. I figured he had probably already boarded, "Hell, nothing beats a failure but a try," I thought, as I dialed the number. Just as I expected, he had already boarded his plane, and there would be no last kiss for us in Kansas City.

I sat impatiently tapping my armrest. "Forget this," I mumbled and called Everett's cell phone once again. When he answered, I asked,
"Do you mind getting off your plane to give me a kiss?"
"Kyra, are you serious?"
" Yes, I'm very serious, please get off your plane?"
"Do you really want me to?"
"Yes, I want you to, or I wouldn't have called."
"Okay, I'm getting off right now."

I unfastened my seatbelt, and exited the plane. Once I made it through the doors, there stood Everett at the counter. I ran up to him and hugged his neck, while expressing how much I cared about him.

He put his finger on my lips to quiet me and tenderly kissed them. He slightly backed away, looked into my eyes and stated, "You are so beautiful! Someone once told me that black diamonds were very beautiful. I just never knew how beautiful they were until you became a part of my life. Kyra, my black diamond, I love you so much and always will. I'm going to miss you baby, but I'd rather miss you and know that your situation at home was better. I want you to go home and get your marriage together, and if you need me, call me." We hugged one last time, then re-boarded our planes.

20

Manila Envelope

Bruce and Taylor were at the airport waiting when I arrived. I hugged them both and attempted to throw my luggage into the car, but Bruce quickly intervened and insisted that I allow him to help me. I was puzzled. "Bruce wants to help me?" I thought. However, I didn't start in with my sarcasm since all was going so well, and he was trying to have a sensible evening. I thanked him for his assistance and inquired about my car. I had driven myself to the airport, so I was confused as to why he was picking me up.

He stated that he and one of his friends had picked my car up that Friday night and taken it home. I thanked him once again, and since we really didn't share any of the same kinds of interest anymore, I tried to think of some kind of a topic for small talk. I searched my mind for something that would carry us as far as home without starting an argument. I shared with him my thoughts about the families I observed traveling in the airport. I mentioned to him how I sat there wishing that one day he and I could do something as meaningful with Taylor. He agreed that he, too, experienced some of the same thoughts while traveling himself, and he was looking forward to the day we took our daughter on a family vacation.

Maybe something happened while I was away, because he was being far too nice to me. I had to seriously look at him a few times to make sure that he wasn't an imposter. He was either feeling guilty about possibly experiencing a weekend of infidelity himself, or he was as equally interested as I was in repairing our family situation. I was hopeful that he was ready to reconcile our differences, and I think I was possibly even ready to try and forgive him for his affair. All of the bickering and self-isolation over the past few months had taken a toll on me. I was suffering from a case of serious depression and had just about reached my breaking point. I was ready to resolve our differences, and if professional or spiritual counseling was what we needed to make it through this rough time, I was ready to do whatever it took.

We pulled into the garage and unloaded my bags. I expected to walk in the house and find it a mess, but much to my surprise, it was just as clean as I had left it. "Kyra, I'm going to put Taylor to bed, and then we need to talk." Instantly, I grew very concerned about what he might possibly have on his mind that he wanted to share with me. While I waited for him to put the baby to sleep, I unpacked my luggage and turned the water on in the bathtub. Just as I started to undress, he walked into the bathroom and asked me if I was ready to talk. I turned the water off and followed him into the living room. He sat on the couch, and I sat on the edge of the fireplace with my face propped up on my fist, and gave him my undivided attention.

At first, he just looked at me. I felt like he was assessing me and could clearly see through me. After minutes of staring, he finally spoke.

"Kyra, I really don't know where to begin. I guess I need to start off by just apologizing to you for the neglect you have experienced from me lately. I have been under a lot of stress, and my family has suffered as a direct result of what I'm going through. It may not seem like I love you, but I do. I realized how special you are to me, while you were away this weekend. I never really thought about how important your role is to our family until I started thinking about life without you. I don't know what we need to do to get our family back on the right track, but if it's not too late, I want us to try to do something to save our marriage."

"Well, what do you suggest, Bruce? I've spent these past few months thinking of what might help improve our situation, but we seem so distant and so disconnected. At this point, we may be so damaged that we're beyond professional counseling. I am emotionally exhausted from thinking of solutions that could help us. I feel physically and mentally drained from this marriage. There are days when I want to work out our differences, and there are days when I just simply don't give a damn. Some nights I lay in bed wishing I had the courage to just walk away from this madness. However, I think about Taylor and my desire for her to live in a household with both parents present. That thought alone keeps me trying. But you have stolen the joy of what it means to me to be a wife, and I don't know where I truly stand when it comes to working out our marital problems."

"I just want you to consider what you would be giving up if you divorce me, Kyra. Then think about what the baby would be missing out on, if we're living in two separate locations."

"I often think about what I'd be giving up if we divorced, and to be honest, it's not all that bad. Taylor has been the main reason I have remained in this relationship thus far, but I wish it had been you. All I can say Bruce is that I will try. I can't promise anything other than that."

"That's good enough Kyra. We have to start somewhere. Right!"

It seems like a hug or even a kiss would have been appropriate after talking, but neither of us felt that in our spirit. I sat looking at a picture of Taylor on our living room wall for a minute, and when I was certain that he was finished talking, I went back to preparing for my bath. My water had gotten a little cold, and the bubbles were flat. I turned the hot water on to warm the water that was already in the tub and poured in a little more bubble bath. I put a lit candle at the foot of the tub and set the whirlpool timer on fifteen minutes. I turned off the bathroom light, finished undressing and climbed into the tub. I slouched down in the water as low as I could possibly go and closed my eyes. I reflected over the discussion I had with Everett in the airport and then the discussion with Bruce.

I knew that it was really over between Everett and I. Just like that, our good thing had come to an end. It was too late for me to second-guess my decision, although, I was trying to convince myself of a reason to continue my affair with him. I had already sold out on my self-respect, so why not just call him back and say, "Okay, Everett, I changed my mind for the thirty-third time." This would have certainly provided him with the opportunity to see the confused state of mind I faced on a daily basis. But I knew I couldn't call Everett because I had to give my marriage one last try. I realized that continuing my interaction with him would only complicate my life even more. I knew that keeping him as a part of my inner circle would only prevent Bruce from ever being able to do anything right to please me. And every attempt on his behalf to save our family would always lack something. For that reason alone, I had to discontinue everything Everett and I shared, in order to be fair to my husband and our family.

I sat in the tub for the longest just thinking. I yawned a few times because I was exhausted. My water had gotten ice cold, my candle had almost burned completely down to nothing, and my bubbles were practically gone. I fumbled around in the water feeling for my washcloth, which was caught underneath my leg. I lathered it with soap and bathed. Once I was completely clean, I stepped out of the tub and dried off. While standing by the sink, I noticed Bruce and Taylor already sleeping in our bedroom. I sat the lotion on the edge of the counter and tip-toed into the room, pulling my nightgown over my head. I pulled back the covers on my side and got into bed. I laid there for the longest watching the ceiling fan rotate until I finally fell asleep.

The next morning I got out of bed early. My eyes were red, due to a long and restless night. Thoughts of Everett immediately invaded my mind as I prepared for work. I moved about the house rather slowly all morning and poured myself a glass of orange juice hoping it would give me a burst of energy, but that didn't seem to help.

I drove to work in a daze that morning, and while I sat in rush hour traffic, I wondered if Everett would call as usual to say hello.

I hoped he would, but I figured he would attempt to honor my request, so I wasn't expecting him to call.

I made it into my office about nine-thirty, and before I sat my purse down on my desk, I pressed my speakerphone to check my messages. There were three messages on my voice mail, none of which were from Everett. "He's not going to call," I thought to myself. "Well Kyra, this is what you wanted," my conscience reminded me. But, that didn't change the fact that I wanted to say hello to him or hear his voice. That had been my Monday morning routine for months. I thought about calling him a few times, but after my discussion with Bruce, I owed it to him not to. He had made a sincere plea to me about our marriage, and I was going to try hard to honor his request.

I turned on my computer, sat at my desk and rested my head against my high back chair. I closed my eyes and attempted to clear my thoughts. But, the more I tried to redirect my thoughts, the harder it was for me to concentrate on anything else. My cell phone rang, and I snatched it up immediately looking at the ID screen. It was Bruce, and he probably didn't want anything, so instead of answering, rushing him off the line or being short with him, I just didn't answer at all. I didn't feel much like talking to him and he would have sensed it in my voice.

My department was preparing for an audit and nothing was going to be accomplished with me just sitting there, so I pulled out a few files and attempted to do a little work for the day. Just as I started to get busy, Gail popped her head in my office door.

"Hey Kyra, how was your weekend?" She asked.
"It was ok. How was yours?
"It wasn't too bad. I didn't do too much, just sat around. You know there's not much for a single sista to do outside of work. That's why you need to hook me up with that cousin of yours. "
"Oh okay." I replied in a most distracted manner.

"Kyra are you doing ok. You have really been acting different for the past few months. I'm worried about you. You just don't seem happy lately."

"Girl, I'm just going through some things. Don't worry about me. I'll be ok." I said, while partially smiling at her.

"You know if you need to talk, I'm here for you."

"Yeah I do, thanks Gail."

Gail hugged me and exited my office, leaving my door half open. Her hug seemed to help a bit, but it still wasn't enough to make me stop thinking about Everett.

The time I spent talking to Gail, and the Mr. Barnett distractions I kept having, prevented me from accomplishing any work. By four that evening, I had only completed one file. On an average day, I would have been much more productive, but this wasn't an average day, so I hadn't accomplished a damn thing. I realized that I wasn't going to either, so I decided to go home early, cook dinner and spend time with my family. On my way to the elevator, Gail yelled for me to wait. She approached me and handed me a large manila envelope.

"What is this?" I asked.

"I don't know. It was delivered certified mail for you Friday. Since it was addressed to you and marked confidential, I didn't open it."

"Well thanks." I replied, as I took the envelope and entered the elevator. I started to open it when I got to my car, but because I assumed that it was business related, I sat it on the passenger seat and drove home.

When I made it home, Taylor was still at the sitters and Bruce was out with friends watching a game. I had picked up a bottle of wine and some fruit to surprise him. It was my plan to have dinner waiting when he came home, like old times. I intended to prepare a fruit salad for later that evening, and drink a glass of wine with him by the fireplace in our den after the baby went to sleep.

While I was cooking, Bruce called to say that he was going to be in late. He claimed that he had to meet with some co-workers to prepare a presentation for the following afternoon in Houston. I instantly became defensive, because I had no trust in him at all. He clearly could have been conducting business, but because our trust had been so violated, I thought he was conducting more of a late night booty call. I said exactly that to him, and I hung up the phone.

I finished cooking dinner and decided to pick Taylor up from the sitter's house at about six-thirty. As I processed our conversation from the night before, I couldn't believe that the day after we talked about making our marriage work, he was already calling home with excuses. "This is exactly why nothing good is going to happen between Bruce and I," I screamed while backing my car out of the garage. In the past, all it would have taken for me to call Everett was something as small as Bruce's calling home to say he would be out late. I had gotten so used to calling him for everything over the past few months, so it was very difficult not to call him for comfort. Though I knew he wouldn't reject me, I wanted to do what was fair for both of us, so I didn't call at all, but it was rather hard not to.

While the garage was closing, I noticed the envelope sitting on my seat. I snatched it out of anger while harshly stating, "What the hell is this," as I opened the envelope. Enclosed, was an additional envelope, a folder and a letter. I opened the folder and read the letter. It read,

"Mrs. Murrell,
I called you almost two weeks ago about your case with our company. I mentioned that I had photos for you; however, you never scheduled a time with me to pick them up. I sent them certified mail to your office to prevent them from being intercepted by your husband. If you have any additional questions, please feel free to contact me. Thank you for your business.

Herbert Perkins, Investigator
CEO, Perkins Enterprise."

My heart started pounding fast, as I considered whether I should even open the additional envelope that contained the photos. I stared at the envelope, as tears fell from my eyes. I finally had to deal with the reality of Bruce cheating on me. I wasn't ready to know who the other woman was, so I put everything back in the folder and threw it on my passenger seat. I shifted the gear to reverse and backed out of the driveway. I drove as far as the corner and the suspense was killing me. I had to know who Bruce's mistress was. I reached over, opened the envelope and started screaming like a fucking maniac. "No Bruce! Nooooooo!" I screamed, while crying uncontrollably and beating the steering wheel. "This can't be real. This.... can't ....be..... real," I kept repeating. My heart had just been ripped out of my chest.

Bruce was having an affair with Gail and all that time I never suspected a thing. But now I understood. Once I replayed in my mind her current need to be around me all the time. I clearly understood her demeanor in trying to get closer to me. I understood why she was always in my business, why she was always asking me about my plans for the weekend, and why I was so depressed.

It finally clicked that Gail was only doing what snake bitches do, when they are after your man, and trying to keep you in the dark. She had done such an excellent job at it as well, which made me very angry. But, understanding and knowing the truth wasn't a good thing for her because now I wanted to confront her ass. I reached for my cell phone, called the babysitter and told her I would be late.

I drove to Gail's house only to discover Bruce's platinum, S Class, Mercedes in her driveway. I couldn't believe it. "Working late," I uttered to myself, as I opened my car door and popped my trunk. "Working late." I repeated, as I walked to the back of my car and pulled out my crow bar. "Working late." I stated one last time, as I walked up to his car and scratched the hell out of it from one end to the other. I raised the crowbar and considered breaking out his windows, but that might have been a dead give away that I was there, and I wanted to surprise them.

The sun was setting when I walked up on Gail's porch. I remember thinking how beautiful it was, considering, it was one of the worst days of my life. I gripped my crowbar in my right hand tightly and rang the doorbell with my thumb. I braced myself and tried to calm my nerves, as I waited for someone to open the door.

I could hear Gail twist the lock from the inside, which made me open the screen door. I wanted to make sure that I got into the house, once the door was opened and she discovered that I was on the other side. She never bothered to look out the window, nor did she inquire as to whom was at the door. When she opened it, she had the most pleasant look on her face, until it registered in her mind that I was standing in her presence.

"My God! Kyra! What are you doing here?" She asked, with this mystified look on her face.

"Bitch! Where's my husband. Tell Bruce to get his ass to the door right now. Better yet. Move the hell out of my way!" I screamed while pushing her aside and walking into her house.

"Bruce, I know your punk ass is in here. You better come out here right now before I do some major damage up in here." I screamed once I got into the house.

"Kyra, please allow me to explain," Gail quickly suggest.

"You must be a fool to think that you could give me a reasonable explanation as to why my husband is in your house. Have you lost your mind?"

Just as I was walking up on Gail, Bruce walked in from the kitchen in his T-shirt. His slacks were slightly unzipped and his shoes were off. His being half dressed caught me totally off guard, which caused me to stare him up and down. Once it was clear that I saw what I thought I saw, I went into a raging fit and slapped the hell out of him.

"You sorry BASTARD! How could you stoop so low? How could you do this to me? How could you do this to our family? How could you cheat on me with my damn co-worker?

"Kyra, ...Baby."

"Baby! Don't "baby" me. You have obviously lost it too. You are another woman's house in your T-shirt and socks, with your pants unzipped, and you think you can call me "baby." What the hell are you doing here Bruce?"

"I know I'm out of line for being here, and I know that this doesn't look right, but I can explain."

"Well you better have a hell of an explanation for me then. Because I can't think of any acceptable reason for you to have your black ass here."

"Kyra, Gail and I have been seeing each other for over eight months. I was here ending our relationship tonight. I told her that I wanted to work on getting my family back in order and she understands that I'm not going to be seeing her any longer."

"Kyra, Bruce and I are ending our relationship and I'm so sorry about this." Gail stated while trying to approach me.

"Bitch! Shut up talking to me and back the hell up. You betrayed me. You smiled in my face everyday, pretending to be my friend. You made it seem as though you were so concerned about me and you're sleeping with my husband on the down low. When were you going to tell me about that, Gail? When were you going to sit down in my office, smile in my damn face like you do all the time and tell me that you've been screwing my husband? It's a good thing that you didn't know the envelope you gave me this afternoon consisted of photos of you and Bruce. Had you known, I might still be in the dark. Gail, there's nothing you can say to me that would change my mind about the bullshit I'm seeing right now."

"Kyra, I am your friend, I just got caught up in the moment and let my loneliness get the best of me."

"And now it's about to get you whipped. Gail, I'm not thinking clearly right now.......... Stop talking to me before I snap and put your ass on life support. You were never my friend because friends don't sleep with each other's husbands."

"Kyra, I'm so sorry." She stated one more time before I lost it all together. I started walking up on her because I felt betrayed, but Bruce grabbed me, and I instantly started screaming at her.

"Gail you are sorry and you can't explain anything to me. I knew I needed to be leery of you after I got promoted over you. It was so obvious from day one, but I wanted to give you the benefit of doubt. Friends don't hurt friends like this.....And Bruce you are even sorrier for stooping this low. What have I done to deserve this from you?"

"Kyra, calm down baby and let me talk to you." He stated.

"Calm down! Calm down! I walk up in another woman's house and find my husband chillin, and you're telling me to calm down. I'm not calming down, nor am I discussing anymore of our family business in front of your bitch. Let me go right now Bruce before I hurt you."

"I'm not letting you go until you calm down. Just listen to me for a second and I'll let you go."

"Fuck that! I'm not talking to you about anything pertaining to our marriage in front of this woman. Get your shit and let's go right now."

Gail and Bruce both looked shocked when I informed him to get his things. She probably thought I was going to take him home and kill his sorry ass. But neither of those losers was worth my serving fifty years to life over.

While I stood waiting in Gail's living room, I watched Bruce walk to the back of her house to get his belongings. I was breathing hard and trying to calm my nerves. But, just as I was about to calm down, I noticed a framed snapshot sitting on her glass entertainment center. "I'll be damned," I mumbled. The photo was of her and Bruce and had been taken in my house some time in December because my Christmas decorations were up. I walked over to the entertainment center, which Gail was standing by, looked a little closer at the photo and turned into an instant lunatic on her. I grabbed her by her hair with my left hand and the two of us fell up against the couch. I was still holding my crowbar, and when I lifted it to hit her, Bruce ran back into the living room and grabbed me. All I remember after that was swinging my crowbar at him and a few sounds of shattering glass followed. Gail's entertainment center was destroyed, and I had no remorse about my actions.

Bruce carried me out of Gail's house, while attempting to keep us apart. He told her to go back into the house a few times because he was trying to defuse the situation. Once he got me out to my car, he angrily ordered me to get in and shut the door. Gail came back out on her porch screaming at me. "Kyra, if you had done your job as a wife in the first place, I wouldn't have been playing your role to begin with."

The last thing I needed was her pouring salt in my wounds, so I responded just as ignorant as she had. "Whatever Bitch! If you had done your job as a wife to begin with, you would still be with your own damn husband instead of mine and your ex-husband wouldn't now be your brother-in-law. So I guess your sister gave you the same advice you're giving me. But, what I'd advise you to do is stop talking to me before I come up on that porch and fuck you up," I replied, while starting my car. It was clearly obvious to me that we had both reverted back to our past upbringing in the hood and had become straight ignorant in her exclusive neighborhood, and if Bruce followed me home, I was taking it to mine.

Bruce intervened right about the same time he noticed the deep scratch on his car. He angrily yelled, "Kyra, stay in your car and leave. Gail be quiet and go back in the house." I looked at Bruce like he was foolish and then sped off. I observed him backing out of her driveway in my rear view mirror and shortly after, he pulled up right behind me. I'm sure a number of thoughts crossed his mind, as we drove down Gail's street. But I was numb to his emotions. I didn't care if he was embarrassed about my behavior or mad about his car being scratched up. A woman could only endure so much, and I had exceeded my level of tolerance. He called my cell phone and asked me to go home before picking up Taylor because he didn't want to hash out our problems in front of her, and I was fine with that.

Once we made it home, I pulled in the driveway, and he pulled up next to me. He got out of his car and assessed the damage I had done. While he was bent over rubbing the scratch, I walked over to him screaming and crying. I started hitting him and asking him "Why would you do something like this to our family?" He grabbed my arms and tried to move me into the garage because my neighbor was taking out his trash and noticed us fighting. Bruce looked over at him, and shook his head in disgust, as he picked me up and physically carried me into the garage. He was totally embarrassed, and I didn't give a damn. As the garage closed, he asked me one last time "Kyra, please calm down." But as hurt as I was, I don't even think that was an option for him at the time.

21

Ultimate Breaking Point

Once we got inside the house, Bruce explained to me that he never intended to get romantically involved with Gail. He told me that he had gone out a few times with some of his frat brothers and saw her at the sports bar. One night he bought her a few drinks, while they sat around talking about the struggles of relationships and things seemed to blossom from there.

They exchanged numbers, and one weekend when she knew I was out of town, she called him and invited him out for a drink. The first few times they went out were quite innocent, but because I had shut him off sexually, she eventually provided that kind of fulfillment for him as well. One encounter led to another and she started to take a few romantic trips with him. When he was away on business, she would generally fly out on the weekends after work and they would rendezvous wherever he was assigned for that week. Sometimes they would fly back together early that following Monday morning. She would go to work, and he would go to her place and lounge until later that evening. Then later that night, he would come home acting as though he had just gotten in from the airport.

He claimed he had gone over to her house that Monday evening with every intention on terminating their relationship, but she asked him if they could have one last evening together, and he agreed. She cooked him dinner, and they talked. He assured me that they had not been intimate that night, but she wanted to. He said he talked with her about the discussion we had the night before, and our plans to reestablish our family. He told her that he wanted to honor the commitment we made that Sunday night to work out our problems. But actually, I could have cared less about him not sleeping with her that night. For some reason all the times he had slept with her prior to that moment stood out most in my mind.

The real bombshell occurred when she confirmed for him that I was not away on company business the weekend I went to Kansas. He also explained that after she told him my news, it was unbearable for him to envision me with another man, which was one of the reasons he called so much while I was away. I looked at him like "yeah right," and he started divulging his pain.

"Kyra I realized what I was about to lose, which is why I picked you up from the airport and talked with you about making our marriage right again. After Gail mentioned that your trip wasn't a business trip, I became unfocused on the evening she and I were trying to have. I almost lost it when I envisioned another man holding you in his arms and discontinued all the plans she and I had for the remainder of the weekend. I needed to think about what I was sacrificing, how I could get myself together and what I could do to make you fall in love with me again. I would be lying if I said I didn't love you or I didn't care about what has happened to our family. It troubles me more than you realize. So, how can we make our situation right again? And baby, I desperately need to know if you're have having an affair, and if so, with who?"

Bruce knew he couldn't take the truth, and his tears didn't seem to move me one bit. As bad as I was hurting, I wanted to scream, " Hell Yeah! I'm cheating on you," in order to pour salt in his wounds. But since he had no concrete evidence to verify his speculations, there was no need to admit to anything. As far as I was concerned, I was the victim in this situation, and since I had the evidence to prove his infidelity, I didn't say one word to convict myself. How was he going to try and turn this mess around on me when he was the guilty one? I was hurting after I caught my husband with a woman I considered to be my friend. Gail and I had worked together for over eleven years. I had befriended this woman and promoted her to my Assistant Director when other administrators didn't believe in her professional abilities.

How the two of them could do this and feel no shame about it baffled me. I wasn't ready to resolve anything with Bruce, so I told him I needed some time to be alone to really think about my next move. He agreed to move in with his sister, until we decided what we were going to do about our marriage. He packed a few of his personal items in a small travel bag and left. He insisted that I not worry about picking Taylor up that evening because he would get her in route to his destination.

When he left, I watched him back out of the driveway and accepted the fact that what we once shared might never exists again. To some degree, we had both fallen out of love with each other. We had moved on in our intimate lives with someone else and totally violated our marital vows and our pledge to each other before God, our family and friends. And though I knew committing adultery with Everett was clearly wrong, some good had come out of my affair with him for me. He had taken the time to become my friend and encouraged me in everything that mattered in my life to me. No matter how big or small, he always got excited about every issues pertaining to me, which is exactly what I needed.

Initially, I believed that Bruce's deceitful behavior is what destroyed our home. I concluded that because of his infidelity, he failed to live up to my expectations of him as a husband. When I considered the encounter we had at Gail's house, I thought of the saying "What you do in the dark, will eventually come to light." Well the light came crashing in on him, and it definitely affected me, which is why I finally reached a point in my life where I didn't care any longer about saving my marriage. My daughter, my sanity, and my self-dignity were the only points that mattered to me now.

I tried to figure out what I had done to fail Bruce as a wife. I kept asking myself, "What in the world had I possibly done to drive him into the arms of another woman? Where did we go wrong and why did we openly invite outsiders into our marriage?" We had been such a happy loving couple. However, somewhere down the line, we started to live a lie that we, unfortunately, never escaped and the consequences of our actions was costly.

When I thought about it, I couldn't even figure out how or when the crisis in our lives began, and in trying to do so, I became highly depressed. The reality of Bruce's affair became more than I could endure, and I almost couldn't function. I stayed home from work for the rest of the week, sitting around in the dark. Taylor stayed with Bruce those first few days, so I was home alone. Home alone with nothing but idle time to think about my sorrows. I spent hours reflecting over my past experiences, past relationships, past male role models and my level of disappointment in the males in my life in general. From my Daddy to Bruce, every significant male in my life had disappointed me. How hopeless and let down I was feeling. What I realized in a matter of a few months was that I had allowed myself to become completely consumed with depression about my entire life.

I realized that God, friendship, honesty, trust and teamwork was initially the perfect formula for my relationship with Bruce. Once a little of each started to dwindle, our marriage became a real disaster. From that first disagreement with Bruce in July of 2000 to present, I had finally reached my point of no return. I had come to a point in my life where I frequently contemplated suicide to the extent of needing to act upon it. That Thursday evening, I found myself slumped over the edge of the bed. My face and eyes were slightly swollen from crying all day. "Shit, Kyra, get yourself together," my conscience insisted. There I was with a glass of wine and thirty-five pills in my hand ready to end it all. "Are you seriously going to kill yourself and leave Taylor here with Bruce and his bitch to raise her?" I asked myself.

Tears started to flow uncontrollably from my eyes, as I acknowledged that I had definitely reached my lowest of low's, my weakest of weak, my ultimate breaking point. I didn't have any kind of direction for my present situation and no vision for my tomorrow, which wasn't normal for me. I was a blissful dreamer, a visionary, a go-getter, a mover and a shaker. Now, here I was at a point in my life with nothing more going for myself than the struggles of a bad marriage and the misery that came along with it.

Life had become so bleak for me, and I was very disappointed with the example my marriage had been for my daughter. Our present family environment wasn't what I wanted for her for the next sixteen years either. I knew she deserved something far better from us both, but making it happen seemed impossible.

If Bruce had to move out and we had to live in two separate households to provide her with stability, then a separation would be well worth it for my health and sanity. I should have left Bruce when our situation initially got unbearable, but everyone had such high expectations of me. How do you go to your family, friends and the people who look up to you and tell them that you and your mate strongly dislike each other and have for years? How do you tell your family that your marriage is a living hell or that it's not working out at all, when everyone in the family sees you as the shining star? I had convinced myself that it was almost impossible for me to share that kind of information with anyone because everyone expected so much from Kyra Murrell, the skinny little educated sista, with the over achiever attitude.

Unfortunately, I had tolerated Bruce's mess for so long to maintain my rich girl; I done made it over image that I worked so hard to establish for myself. I now realize that it was simply not worth it since the stressors of maintaining our relationship led me to a place in my life I never wanted to venture. The stress from the entire situation had me so worn down that not only did I loose major weight, but I started to look and feel like shit every time I looked in a mirror. The sexy diva I once saw when I passed mirrors had vanished right before my very eyes. She no longer existed and what bothered me most was that I didn't know where to start looking to find her again.

175

"What is killing yourself going to prove?" I asked myself, and there were no answers for such a foolish act. The only rational thing I could think of was my child. When people spoke of her Mom, I didn't want Taylor to have to explain why I killed myself for the rest of her life.

My rational inner being took advantage of that one sane moment and encouraged me by saying, "Wipe your eyes, put down those pills, that wine, get out of this damn house and go get some professional help right now." I sat my glass of wine on the entertainment center at the foot of my bed, walked into the bathroom and flushed my pills down the toilet. Tears continued to pour from my eyes, as I grabbed my car keys and set the house alarm.

Once I made it into the garage, I sat in my car trying to get myself together enough emotionally to drive. I noticed the photos of Bruce and Gail still sitting on my passenger seat. I started my car and hesitantly opened my garage door. I briefly considered leaving it closed and killing myself by carbon monoxide poisoning. I knew it would destroy Bruce to come home and find me dead in the garage. Then I thought, "But what if Taylor were with him and saw me that way. I wouldn't want her to experience anything like that and remember it for the rest of her life."

The more I thought about killing myself, the more I realized that my motives were all for the wrong reasons. It was all about revenge, just like my affair had been. I was aching inside, and I wanted Bruce to hurt in the same manner in which he had hurt me. I wanted him to live the rest of his life remembering the sacrifice he made when he chose everything else over our family. I wanted him to know that no matter what he did in life, I would always have the satisfaction of making him remember what he had in me, how he drove me crazy, what he lost when I died, and the haunting memories of walking up on sudden death. I knew there was no real clarity in my thinking, due to my despair. I was pitiful, and in desperate need of help.

I shifted my gear into reverse and backed my car out of the garage. As the door was closing, I reached for my cell phone. I had to call the one companion in my life who was always so warm, patient and gentle with me over the past few months, Everett.

During my first attempt to reach Everett, his cell phone rang six times and on the seventh ring, I heard a woman's voice say,
"Hello."
"Hello." I repeated.
"Yes may I help you?"
"I'm sorry, I must have the wrong number." I replied.
"Ok." She stated and hung up.

"I know Kimberlin isn't answering Everett's phone," I thought to myself. "Or maybe he saw my number and told her to answer." "No Kyra. Stop tripping, Everett wouldn't do you like that," my conscience replied. Because I knew he wouldn't intentionally avoid me, I tried to call a second time and the outcome was pretty much the same.

"Hello," she stated.
"Yes, I was trying to reach Everett, I must have the wrong number."
"No, you have the right number," she replied in a polite tone.
"Well who is this?" I asked.
"Kimberlin, Everett's fiancé. May I take a message?"
"His fiancé," I thought before replying. "Oh, hi Kimberlin. This is Kyra, would you tell Everett I called please?"
"Kyra, is this his cousin Kyra, from Oklahoma?" She eagerly asked.
"His cousin!!!!!! What the hell?" I quickly whispered to myself, before replying, "Yes, yes this is."
"It's nice to finally speak with you. Everett talks about you all the time. He told me that you and your daughter were just in town last month visiting his Mom right before the holidays. Sorry I didn't get a chance to meet you, but I was having some complications

from my pregnancy, and my doctor wouldn't let me leave Chicago until the week before Christmas."

"PREGNANCY!!!!!"...raced from one side of my brain to the other, and my ego was crushed. I wanted to just hang up in her face because I couldn't play the game any longer. Instead, I mentioned that Everett shared their news and congratulated her.

"When is the baby due?" I asked
"Some time in February, and girl I'm ready," she stated.
"Well congratulations again." I said one last time before experiencing a brief moment of silence. Finally, I said, "Girl, I'm going to get off this phone. You take care and tell Everett I said hey."

Speaking with Kimberlin made me even more anxious to talk with Everett. He never left his phone at home and here I was at my most desperate point in life getting more bad news. He had truly played the cousin role to a T. And here I was thinking for months that I was the only one benefiting from that damn cousin game. He had taken our little fictitious family relationship home, and was using it to his advantage as well. I felt highly deceived, and I wanted to curse him out about lying to me.

All that time this man had been talking about how much he loved me for months, but neglected to tell me that he was engaged to be married, and that his woman was about to give birth to his baby that following month. All I could ask myself was, "How did I allow myself to be played so foolishly by a man that I knew was clearly involved with someone else." I had plenty of time to save myself from this unnecessary heartache, but my loneliness kept telling me to go forth, and I did like a damn fool.

After I got Everett's news, I knew I couldn't return home. I needed some professional help for the depression I was experiencing. I called two facilities and someone answered the hotline to the second facility on the first ring. I spoke with the hotline operator and shared with her a few of the burdens I was dealing with. She listened and spoke with such compassion. She asked me to come to the hospital and meet with one of the clinical professionals they had on staff, and I agreed. She stayed on the line with me as I drove to the hospital and then walked over to the emergency admittance area to assist me with checking in. **Grace** was her name. She didn't look anything like I envisioned either, but this soft-spoken; six-foot tall woman had just initiated the first phase of helping me save the rest of my life.

As I proceeded with the intake process and saw my doctor for the first time, I felt like a real psycho after getting an actual DSM-IV Psych diagnosis. However, I tried to make myself recognize that there were far worse titles I could have carried in life besides the one of Depressive Disorder. I also told myself that this diagnosis was not the problem, but part of the solution for me to start living life to the fullest once again.

Spending time in the hospital gave me an opportunity to focus on Kyra, and what I wanted out of life for myself. The days I spent processing with my therapist helped me realize that until I started to focus on the real issues that disrupted my home, there would never be any room for growth. What I discovered while processing with Dr, Holloway was that I brought baggage into my marriage when I avoided taking some time for closure after Calvin and I separated. All the trust issues I had with him, all the heartaches, all the inappropriate behaviors he exemplified, and the disappointment of our failed relationship dwelled in my heart and mind. I never gave myself time to heal, so me unconditionally trusting Bruce never stood a chance to begin with.

Once I left the crisis center, my life seemed to have real purpose again. I had a genuine sense of peace about the issues I encountered and a plan to make things better for myself. Once I talked with Everett about his marital proposal to Kimberlin and the baby they were expecting, I understood the real degree of deception which occurred between us. He had intentionally taken advantage of my vulnerability, and lured me in when I was most desperate for companionship. And though he should have never been what I used as a quick solution for my marital problems, I was weak, and highly confused at the time we became involved.

It was ludicrous for me to even consider an extra marital affair at all. I knew that most affairs were often short term and generally served as band-aids. I admit that I truly went wrong when I looked for temporary satisfaction outside of my marriage. But sometimes when your life is lacking something you feel you need, deserve, or want, it's virtually impossible to just do without. I had become so co-dependent on Everett when my marital problems became unbearable, that I neglected to call on the only spiritual being that had never let me down. "My Heavenly Father."

I now realize that happiness is not based on maintaining two relationships for balance. After living without Bruce for over a year now, I see that we both experienced a great sacrifice because of our infidelity. There are days when I really miss him, the great relationship we used to share and the joys of having a family. However, as bad as I want to honor my wedding vows and forgive him, the human side of me frequently reminds me that he cheated on me first and violated our sacred relationship. And though I cheated as well, the slap in the face I encountered from both Bruce and Everett helped me realize that "Every dog truly has his or her day." Yes, even me, the classy Mrs. Kyra Williams-Murrell had to pay for my actions.

I really don't have all the answers for resolving my situation; however, I try to remain hopeful. I occasionally refer back to my granny's words of wisdom in hopes of one day mending my relationship with Bruce. "*Marriage is a lifetime commitment, hard work and a level of dedication.*" I must admit that I truly didn't understand what she meant, until I had the chance to experience it for myself. Being deceived like I was, was a certain blow beneath the belt. There are days when I can't comprehend how women forgive and forget when they have been cheated on and taken for granted. It has been a real struggle for me to forgive Bruce, but I'm glad I finally decided to share my story in detail with the group today because I hope to find forgiveness and closure within myself.

I keep trying to move on with my life, but guilt and pain has prevented me from successfully doing that. The consequences of my actions have been heavy to bear. I have learned that there is nothing valid enough to make me compromise my morals again. I honestly desire to transform my life and rebuild my self-respect. I believe the solutions to my problems are based on my actions from this point forward. In order to fall in love with Kyra Murrell again, I now know that I have to work on my issues first; therefore, the only things I can do is repent and trust God to work out the rest.

Ladies, I apologize for my action earlier. My failure to celebrate your news this morning wasn't about you Carla; it was about my personal degree of pain and resentment. And although I have disclosed my very own story of marital deception, I am still hurting deeply inside. I'm still holding on to lots of heartaches that I must resolve, and until then, my weeping will endure throughout the night, I'll continue to soil pillowcase after pillowcase, but I believe "JOY" for Mrs. K. Murrell is coming in the morning.

Afterword

"Some of the same things that make you laugh, will also make you cry." Most often we don't feel the real repercussions of our negative behavior until it slaps us back in the face. As long as we can be deceitful, but not be deceived, all is well. However, as soon as we have to start reaping what we have sown, it doesn't feel quite the same as when we were dishing it out. There are no happy endings to romantic affairs, only hard feelings, tremendous sacrifices and rude awakenings.

Because we have lived in a "Dog eat Dog" society for some time, deceitful behavior seems normal. Many who have been cheated on, spend the remainder of their time involved in a bad relationship seeking revenge. Some will go to such drastic measures to be victorious, that no one wins in the end.

Committed relationships, however, are realistically meant to be win-win situations, which is why we get romantically involved in the first place. Men and women alike must realize that a commitment is a binding pledge to their mate that is meant to unite them as one. I believe what individuals do to honor their mate and the obstacles they overcome to uphold their pledge is a true reflection of their unconquerable character and their dedicated zeal to make their relationship last forever.

About the Author

Crystal Perkins-Stell was born April 5TH in Newark, New Jersey and raised in Detroit, Michigan. As an adolescent, she was a dreamer, and a visionary who always wrote short stories. She always vowed to her mom that one day she would do big things in life with her creative skills and here she is a few decades later making her dreams a reality.

Crystal completed her Undergraduate Degree at Langston University with scholastic honors and her Masters Degree in Human Relations, with and emphasis in professional counseling from the University of Oklahoma, where she graduated Summa Cum Laude. She became a member of Delta Sigma Theta Sorority Inc., and from past role models and other successful members of her organization, she learned that life is what you make of it. She believes that if you're going to dream, dream big because even if you miss your mark, you'll still be among the courageous individuals labeled as winners for their effort.

In the 90's, Crystal wrote several short stories and poems, which led to her being introduced to NFL players, Kenny Blair and Ron Fellows. They both admired Crystal's talent and allowed her to participate in a project they were doing for the AIDS Foundation. Crystal along with two other local lyricists wrote and performed a song entitled, "The Magic Touch, which they dedicated to Magic Johnson. In the 90's, she also wrote a campaign song for the Oklahoma State Senate Election for the first, black, female, federal judge currently serving in the United States, the Honorable Vickie Miles-Lagrange.

In 2001, after meeting her biological father for the very first time, she started writing her first novel entitled, "456 Fairmont Avenue." However, after encountering personal struggles with their relationship, she lost her zeal for that story and discontinued working on the novel. A year later, her desire to write again was rekindled by a commencement address given by Tom Joyner to Langston University's graduating class. Mr. Joyner's words were sharp and they pierced into Crystal's life like a guided beam of light. "WHAT YOU GON DO NOW," was the question Mr. Joyner's presented to the graduates....Crystal Perkins-Stell replied, "Write a book Tom." That was just the kind of response one would expect from such a blissful dreamer.

Mrs. Perkins-Stell started working on her second book entitled, "Soiled Pillowcases...A Married Woman's Story," and organized, Crystell Publications, Marketing and Distributions, Inc., a sole proprietorship, to publish her first novel. She is now on a mission to make her daring dream, an adventurous and successful accomplishment.

Crystal's next book, "Never Knew A Father's Love," is currently under construction. She is sure that this novel will also be a book reader's are guaranteed to enjoy.